A CHRISTMAS *Charade*

A Novella

—SMALL TOWN CHRISTMAS—
BOOK 2

❄ ❄ ❄

D. ALLEN

DN Publishing

A Christmas Charade
Small Town Christmas, Book 2
Copyright © 2018 by D. Allen
Batavia, NY

www.DavidNethBooks.com

ISBN: 978-1-945336-60-7
First edition

Subscribe to the author's newsletter for updates and exclusive content:
DavidNethBooks.com/Newsletter

Follow the author at:
www.facebook.com/DavidNethBooks
www.twitter.com/DavidNethBooks
www.instagram.com/dneth13

Also by D. Allen

Montana Beach
Summer Stay

Summer Job

Summer Nights

Small Town Christmas
A Christmas Reunion

A Christmas Charade

A Christmas Spark

Standalone
Snow After Christmas

December 19th
Charlotte

The office of *Home & Hearth* magazine is quiet when I get off the elevator. That's never a good sign. With my coffee in one hand and my bag slung over my opposite shoulder, I power-walk to the board room, completely bypassing my desk on the way.

It's already ten after nine and the morning staff meeting is probably already well on its way. Susan Holt, the Editor-in-Chief, is always prompt. I'm not.

When I reach the door, I take a deep breath before quietly pushing it open. Everyone's eyes turn to me as I move to the closest chair. Great.

Without a word, I take my seat next to the new guy. Callum or Jaden or something like that. I don't know. I've only met him once and have barely talked to him at all. I have, however, noticed that he's very attractive. I guess you'd have to be blind not to see that. His blue striped dress shirt fits snug between his broad shoulders. And, as I take my seat, I note how good he smells too. That's a plus when there's no telling how long Susan will keep us.

I fumble in my bag as she goes on about reader surveys, upcoming stories, and photo shoot schedules. Stuff I'm already aware of since I'm the Senior Editor.

By the time I have my pad of paper in front of me and I'm ready to put my full attention on the meeting, I realize everyone's looking at me again.

"Miss Barlow, are you settled now?" Susan asks impatiently. If she used my last name, she must be serious. She glances at my red and green coffee cup and then back at me. Probably should've left that on my desk to hide the reason I'm late.

"Yes, ma'am," I say with a smile.

"Well, as we've discussed between us before—and prior to your arrival—Janet would like to see the website's numbers increase even further before the end of the year."

Janet's the publisher of the magazine and a step above Susan. She's the boss of all bosses here at the magazine.

Susan asks, "Have you had a chance to read the email I sent this morning?"

I gulp. "No."

She raises her eyebrows. "Well, I thought it'd be a great idea to post short catchy stories next week related to the holiday."

"Next week?" I blurt.

"Is that a problem?" she asks.

"Next week is Christmas."

"Yes and our meeting started at nine o'clock."

Point taken.

She studies me a moment longer to make sure I'm not going to interrupt her further. "These will be shorter pieces—maybe 200 words each, preferably lists—and will go on *Home & Hearth*'s blog. They need to be fast, easy reads. Top ten most romantic Christmas traditions, top five date ideas for the holidays, best and worst Christmas proposals, that sort of thing."

I nod and jot her ideas down. This way, at least, I won't see her eyes boring holes in me. She's mentioned these types of stories before—I've even helped develop similar ones with my editorial team—so this should be a piece of cake.

"I want one posted every day by ten in the morning," she says. "Do you think that's manageable?"

"Yes, ma'am." I keep my eyes on my notepad as I write, *Post by 10 every morning* and circle it. I don't even ask if that means Christmas Day too. It probably does. I should be able to schedule it ahead of time so I can still take the day off.

She lets out a sigh, finally letting a little compassion slip into her voice. She nods to the new guy. "Why don't you and Kaden focus on these posts today and tomorrow before the break?"

That's his name!

"If you're both lucky, you should be able to finish before you leave," she continues.

He nods as he writes his own note. "Okay."

"I think it'd be better if the two of you co-wrote each piece," Susan says. "That would give Kaden some more by-lines and would help alleviate the work for you, Charlotte."

Well, we're back on a first-name basis.

I nod, even though I hate the idea of co-writing. Especially with Kaden. He's the newest person in the editorial department. Whether or not he's a good writer, it'll take time to work on these pieces to correct his style and explain to him how to upload things to the website remotely while making them look good.

Merry Christmas to me.

The meeting moves on without anymore punishments sent my way for being late. Thank God. Susan moves on to pitch stories for the print issue in April, spring stories for the website, and fun social media posts that will engage our audience. Same stuff, different day.

When the meeting is over, I carry my bag and my half-empty coffee to my desk and fire up my computer. I dig through my bag and pull out my water bottle, my notepad from the meeting, and a pen. I glance up and see my friend Amy approaching as I type in my password on my computer.

"Well, Susan certainly showed you no mercy." She plops in her chair at her desk, which is next to mine.

I take a sip from my Starbucks. "I guess I shouldn't have been late."

She rolls her eyes. "When *aren't* you late?"

"Yeah, yeah," I mutter.

"It's kind of funny what she assigned you, though." She scrolls through her emails.

My email login screen pops up and I type in my information. "Why's that?"

"You need to write a bunch of articles about dating and romance. As if you have experience with either."

"I've gone on dates!" I say. "Besides, those were just suggestions."

She gives me a sideways look. "How long's it been since you've gone on a proper date?"

I shrug and turn away. "Not that long."

"Long enough."

"Anyway," I say a bit louder. "How's the baby?" Amy just returned from maternity leave at the beginning of the month.

Her face lights up and she immediately reaches for her phone. "She's getting *so big*!" Sliding her chair over to me, she shoves her phone in my direction and says, "Look at her! Isn't she beautiful?"

She is beautiful and I'm very happy for Amy and her husband, but I've seen so many pictures of the baby. She's only two months old. I'm running out of things to say. I only brought it up to avoid talking about my lack of dates.

"And how's mom doing?" I pass her back her phone

after scrolling through a few pictures of Baby Emily sleeping.

"Tired, but at least tomorrow is our last day here." She leans back in her chair and stares at the ceiling. "I'm glad Janet gave us the week off."

"Yeah, that was nice of her."

With Christmas being in the middle of the week, a lot of people would've taken the time off anyway and those who did come in wouldn't have gotten much done. Better to just have the whole week off, according to Janet. I think she wanted the week off as much as we did.

"Are you going to your parents' in Upstate?" Amy asks.

"*Western* New York," I correct with an eye roll and a grin. Living in New York City, I've gotten used to people ignoring the rest of the state. Here, the universe revolves around "the city."

"Whatever," Amy counters.

"But yeah, I am. My sister's supposed to be driving in from Columbus." She had a baby earlier this year, so I'm sure the baby-craze will follow me home, too.

"That sounds like fun."

"Yeah. I'm excited to see them." I miss my sister, but ever since she got married and started having kids, there's been a bit of a disconnect between us. Less things in common, I suppose.

For the rest of the morning, I get to work on the blog posts for next week, reading similar posts on other websites and reading other lists. By lunch time, I've jotted down several ideas for the week. Happy with my work for the morning, I head to the break room for some fresh coffee.

"Oh, hello."

Kaden surprises me when I walk in. He's the only one here and he's sitting at a small table against the wall. He's hunched over his lunch and scrolling through his phone.

He looks up from his yogurt cup. "Hi."

I walk over to the coffee pot. Empty. I pull out the filter and get a new brew ready.

"How do you like working at the magazine so far?" I ask over my shoulder.

"It's not bad. Everyone seems nice." He pauses, then adds, "Well, for the most part."

I smile. "Susan doesn't like it when people are late… and I tend to have an issue with being punctual."

He grins. "I've noticed."

"Yeah." I fill the filter with water and wait for it to start dripping.

"Are you busy later tonight or even this weekend?" he asks. "I would like to take you to dinner or lunch or something."

Is he serious? Or is this his way of prepping for a New Year's Eve date so I'd be more likely to kiss him when the ball drops? Either way, I have the perfect excuse.

"Oh, no. I'm sorry," I say. "I'm going home for Christmas. I leave Saturday morning." The coffee finally starts to drip. "Besides, I'm not really interested in seeing anyone right now. I appreciate it, though."

If I can work on being on time, I think there's a real shot of me taking Susan's job when she retires in two years. Janet loves me and Susan likes my work. Plus, my articles have a tendency of going viral. I just need to keep my head down and work hard until then.

"I just thought we could talk about those articles Susan assigned us to do together," he says.

I blush and turn back to the coffee. "Oh."

So much for that New Year's Eve theory.

"I already have a few ideas. I thought we could figure out how we want to work on them."

I gather a new cup and other additives, waiting for the drip to stop. "Right. Um…well, like I said, I'm going out of town this weekend."

"Oh." He scoops out the last of his yogurt, tossing it aside without the annoying scraping.

"Don't worry about it," I tell him. "I can handle the articles. I'm not really a fan of co-writing anyway."

He squirms a little in his seat. "It's just that Susan wants us both to have bylines and I'd rather not put my name on something I didn't write."

Finally, the coffee is ready and I fill a cup with the fresh brew. "We'll figure it out. Just enjoy your Christmas. It was nice seeing you." I step out before I can put my foot in my mouth again. Thinking he was asking me out on a date when he just meant to work has to be one of the most embarrassing things to happen to me lately.

Real smooth, Charlotte. Real smooth.

MY PHONE BUZZES on the kitchen island as I finish making dinner. My mother's face pops up on the screen and reminds me that I meant to call her to tell her when my train is coming in.

"Hey, Mom." I pin the phone between my shoulder and ear as I dish myself out a bowl of pasta.

"Hello dear, are you busy?"

"No, just about to sit down to dinner. What's up?" I bring the bowl over to my usual spot on the couch and stare out at the Manhattan lights through the big windows.

"Nothing much. I spent most of the day baking."

I smile. I can picture my mom in her apron moving around the small kitchen I grew up in.

That's different, though. After my sister and I moved out, Mom and Dad sold the house and moved into another one in town. They have a much larger kitchen now. She still bakes, but it's not quite the same.

"I'm sure everything's delicious," I tell her. I stab my fork into my meal and blow on it to cool it. "Can't wait to taste them."

"I've got a special plate made for each of you," she says. "Anyway, I'm calling because your father and I are trying to figure out sleeping arrangements. I was just wondering if you're bringing anyone home with you or if you're still looking for that Mr. Right."

Another hint that I'm basically the only single one in my life. Dateless and desperate, apparently.

"I know you said you were single at Thanksgiving, but I thought maybe in the last month with the holiday magic…well, you know."

"Yeah, I know what you mean." I take another bite to buy some time.

In the last month, the closest thing I've had to a date was that awkward encounter with Kaden at lunch. Amy already yelled at me for turning that down.

No, it's just me this year, is on the tip of my tongue, but I hear commotion on the other end.

My mother squeals with excitement and soon I hear a young voice shouting, "Grandma!"

My sister, Olivia, her husband Arthur, and the kids must've just arrived. Hearing the happy reunion through the phone makes me wish I was already on my way home.

"Hello? Charlotte?" my mother says to me.

"I'm still here, Mom." I pop another bite into my mouth.

"Your sister and the kids have just arrived," she tells me. Just what I figured. "Here, talk to her." In the background I hear in a loud whisper, "It's your sister!"

Before I have a chance to say anything, I hear Olivia's voice on the other end.

"Charlotte?"

"Hey. I hear you guys just got in."

"Yeah, Baby Ken is asleep from the long ride, so

getting him through the night should be fun." She gives a half-hearted chuckle.

"I bet." There's one reason why I'm glad I don't have kids yet. I enjoy my sleep too much.

"Anyway, Madison is really excited to see you. It's been a while and I'd really love for her—both of my kids, actually—to get to know their Aunt Char better. You're coming soon, right?"

Olivia couldn't make it to Thanksgiving because they went to Arthur's family in Virginia. I haven't seen my niece since her birthday party in May.

"Yeah, I should be there Saturday night," I say.

"Just you?" she asks. "Because it'd be great for the kids to get a jump start on getting to know a potential uncle, too." She laughs and adds, "I'm kidding, obviously."

I force a laugh. "Well, look, I've got to go. Tell Mom I'll text her when I leave New York. I miss you and I'll see you this weekend. Give the kids a big hug for me."

"Definitely," she says. "Have a safe trip home. See you soon!"

I toss my phone on the couch cushion next to me and raise my cooling bowl of pasta higher so I can finish it. As I eat, I notice my reflection in the window. More importantly, I notice how quiet my apartment is besides the usual noise from outside.

It's just me here. That's never bothered me before, but hearing the happy reunion at Mom's and the questions about whether or not I've found a boyfriend yet makes me feel like I need one. Not for myself, but for everyone else. Well, maybe a little bit for myself. Maybe even just someone who can pretend whenever they're around my family to get them to back off with the jokes. I have my job. That's enough for me right now. For my family, though, it's not nearly enough.

I scoop the last of my pasta in my mouth and set the bowl down on the glass coffee table.

Where can I find a date on such short notice? Someone I can trust. Someone I know and wouldn't mind spending a week with. Someone who will make my family happy enough to back off.

A guy like that might not even exist, but I need to give it a shot. If nothing else, I know one thing for certain: I need to find a date for Christmas.

DECEMBER 20TH

Kaden

"How are you and Charlotte coming along with those blog posts?" Susan stops at my desk on her way back to her office in the morning. Her short dark hair and the suit that fits snug around her thin frame gives off the impression of a person in power, as she is. I've come to realize that it also makes her quite intimidating, as she also is.

"We've talked about it." I don't want to lie, but I also don't want to tell her that Charlotte basically blew me off yesterday.

Susan smiles. "Good. Charlotte's great at her job, so she should be very helpful to you."

I nod. "Yeah, I've read some of her stuff."

"And she's a hell of an editor too. I expect to see great things from the two of you."

I wait until she's back in her office to lower my shoulders.

I really don't want to talk to Charlotte again about these blog posts, but if I want any chance of working my way up in this industry, I need to be able to deal with people with big egos. I can handle Charlotte.

What stings the most is that she turned me down yesterday when I asked her out on a date. I figured Susan's assignment was the perfect excuse to get to know her, but I guess not. Luckily, I think I managed to recover well enough by making it sound like I had intended to work on the articles.

As if on cue, Charlotte walks by with a fresh cup of coffee in her hands. I swear the girl rarely goes a moment without one. She smiles at me as she passes and my pen slips out of my hand as I hurry to wave to her.

She giggles, but keeps walking. At least she's paying attention now.

Charlotte caught my eye the first day I started here a couple months ago. I was her friend Amy's replacement while she was out on maternity leave. I guess I proved my worth because Amy's back and Susan persuaded Janet to keep me on as a staff writer.

Clearly, none of that has even caused a blip on Charlotte's radar, though. When she's not running back and forth to get coffee—or racing to her desk each morning she's late—she usually has her head down buried in her work. Now she's only noticing me because Susan forced us together—and because I'm awkwardly trying to initiate conversation.

Even though Charlotte said she'd take care of it, I use the rest of the day to flesh out even more ideas for the articles—even writing a couple up that have been churning in my mind. I'll need to run them by Charlotte before I post them, just because Susan wants both of our names on it, but I'm not going to let her push me out of this one.

"Put down the work, newbie!" someone calls to me from down the hall after lunch. "Come enjoy the only party this place holds!"

Right. The office Christmas party. I wonder if I was supposed to bring a gift. Too late now.

I've written two stories and have really solid ideas for three more. I suppose that should be enough for now. Maybe I can finish them tonight while I'm still in the "work" frame of mind.

I smile at Charlotte as she and Amy pass by my desk. She doesn't look up from her phone, though.

I shut down my computer and meet everyone in the front lobby of the office. There's cookie platters spread out on the front counter, a "closed" sign on the door, and groups of people standing around and exchanging gifts.

"Grab a plate and help yourself," Kelly says. She's the receptionist and is the one who sent out the memo about the holiday party.

I grab a small plate and fill it with two cookies. It's been two months since I started and while everyone's friendly, I still wouldn't call any of them my friends. This time of year isn't really my favorite, but with a new job and no plans for next week, it's going to be extra rough.

I spot Charlotte in the corner talking with Amy and bravely make my way over there. It's the last day before the holidays and the first story is due on Monday morning. Something needs to show up on the website or Susan's not going to be happy. Charlotte might have some job security, but as a newbie, I don't.

"Hey," I say as an icebreaker.

She offers a polite smile. "Hey."

"You doing anything fun for Christmas?" Amy asks.

I shake my head. "Not really, no. You?"

"Just spending time with my family," she replies. "It's going to be baby-central with my parents and everyone else."

"My house too," Charlotte adds. "My nephew is only eight months old and he hasn't been home since my niece's birthday in May."

Amy rolls her eyes. "I'm sure you can brave one week with kids."

"You don't like kids?" I ask and immediately regret it. It sounded less aggressive in my head.

"It's not that I don't *like* them, it's just that I'm so accustomed to not having them around, you know?"

"But you're their aunt…" I push. Why can't I stop myself?

She scratches the back of her neck. "Anyway, I'm glad you're here."

I smile, hopeful.

"I've written several of the articles that Janet wants."

My face drops. I should've known.

"I can write up the rest tomorrow on my train ride home and get those uploaded. So you'll be off the hook."

I set the untouched plate of cookies down. "No, *I* already wrote them."

"You did?" She looks surprised.

Amy scoots away. "I'm going to go get something else to eat…"

"I told you I wasn't comfortable putting my name on something I didn't write," I say when Amy's gone.

Charlotte pulls out her phone and gives a heavy sigh when she reads it.

"What?" I ask, realizing how petty it is to argue over bylines. Between the two of us, we've written enough articles. The work is done. We should just upload them with our separate bylines and wait for the wrath of Susan after Christmas.

"Nothing." She locks her phone and looks up at me. "How about you edit my articles and I'll edit yours—not rewrite, just edit—and we'll put both of our bylines on the articles. How's that sound?"

I don't want to agree to it until I've read her articles, but I already know that she's a good writer. She wouldn't have the position she does if she wasn't.

"Okay. Fine. But we both get a final read-through before it's posted, okay?"

She shrugs. "Sure. If you want." Her phone buzzes

again and she looks at it with a frown.

"Are you okay?" I ask.

Slipping her phone in her back pocket, she forces a smile. "Yeah. I've gotta get going. I hope you have a nice Christmas and I'll see you when we get back. Don't forget to send me the files so I can add my personal touch."

She doesn't wait for my response and rushes back toward her desk to grab her things.

"Where's she going?" Amy asks, breaking through the thickening crowd.

"She's leaving."

She gives me a confused look. "I'll go talk to her."

I reach for her to stop her. "No, let me. It must've been something I said that upset her." I know it probably doesn't have anything to do with the blog posts—those are probably furthest from her mind—but now I feel bad for pushing the issue. Still, I replay the conversation in my head and try to figure out what she took offense to.

"Good luck," Amy says.

Charlotte nearly collides into me in the hallway on my way back.

"Are you sure you're okay?" I ask her.

She rubs her forehead. "Yeah. Just…leave me alone. I'll be all right." She weaves through the crowd and out the door.

Quickly, I grab my things and toss a wave to Amy in my pursuit of Charlotte.

The elevator doors are still open by the time I get out there and I manage to step inside.

Charlotte rolls her head back and looks at the ceiling as the elevator doors close. "I was hoping to have a second to myself."

"Look, I'm sorry for bugging you about the bylines," I say. "I was just trying to follow Susan's rules. I didn't mean to add more stress to your life."

She looks confused. "What?"

"You seem like you've got a lot on your mind and I'm sure this new assignment isn't helping," I say. "I thought maybe I could try to alleviate that in some way."

"No, you—" She stops herself and studies me for a moment.

"What?"

She waves it off. "Never mind."

"No, what?"

"What are your plans for Christmas?"

I shrug. "I don't know. Nothing much, really." Nothing at all is more like it.

"You're not spending time with friends or family?"

I shake my head.

"Not going on vacation?"

"No, why?"

"You're not doing *anything* for the holidays?"

I am the epitome of single, so no. But best not to come off desperate, Kaden.

"What are you getting at?"

The elevator doors open on the ground floor and a group of people wait anxiously to enter.

Again, she waves it off. "Never mind."

I follow her through the lobby and out into the cold night.

"You have something to say, so just say it," I push. "Do you need me to work on an article? Furniture moved? Money for a trip? What?"

She scoffs. "I wouldn't ask you for money. I wouldn't put you in that type of situation."

"Then what is it?"

She stops dead in the middle of the busy sidewalk and looks at me. "Are you really free or are you just trying to be nice? I'm serious that I don't want to ruin any plans you might have."

I'm looking at a week of watching Christmas specials that I've already seen this year and buying discounted candy the day after Christmas. I could use an activity to take up a day of doing nothing.

"I really am free."

She considers my response. "Do you want to get Chinese for dinner?"

Well that came out of left field. "Didn't you just tell me yesterday that you didn't want to have dinner with me tonight?"

Charlotte starts walking again. "So I changed my mind. Keep up."

"You're kind of sending me mixed signals here."

"Sorry. I'll explain everything once we get out of the cold."

We pass several Chinese places, but still she keeps on marching. Finally, she pulls out her keys and lets us into a quiet whitewashed lobby with mailboxes lining the walls. She goes to one and pulls out a few letters.

"I thought you wanted food?" I ask.

She hits the button for the elevator. "I like to order from this place on Third. They have *the best* food. It's probably clogging my arteries, but maybe this way my mother won't make a comment about how thin I am when she sees me."

The doors open and we step in. She flips through her mail and I watch the elevator climb to the eighth floor.

Down a narrow hallway, her door sits at the end. She drops her bag on a chair by the door when she steps through and flicks on the lights.

There's a clean white kitchen with stainless steel appliances to the left of the door. Charlotte steps down into the sunken living room that's barely big enough to fit her large white sectional that faces the TV on the wall leading to the bedroom and bathroom.

What catches my attention, though, are the large windows that showcase the city lights. It's much better than my apartment in Queens. Mine's a bit bigger, but hers certainly has more updates.

"Have a seat." She taps away at her phone and pours us each a glass of wine.

I sit on the edge of the sectional and look around. "This is a really nice place."

"Thanks." She hands me my wine and takes a seat on

the opposite end of the couch. Tucking her feet up, she works off each of her shoes and tosses them over the glass coffee table. "The food should be here in ten minutes."

"How much?"

She waves it off. "Nonsense, it was my suggestion. Besides, what I'm about to ask of you is worth way more than a single Chinese takeout meal."

"Okay…" I say slowly, trying not to show how nervous I am at the buildup.

"Yeah."

I take a sip of my wine, hoping it'll help my nerves. This morning I thought Charlotte didn't notice me at all and now I'm sipping wine with her in her living room. "Are you going to tell me what this is all about or are you just going to keep beating around the bush?"

"Well, I thought it'd be better to get some food in us first, but I guess I can tell you," she says.

My mind races as I try to piece together what she could ask. It's not about the blog posts, I know that much. Well, now I do. She seemed bothered by whatever she read on her phone in the office. And she mentioned something about her mother.

"I need a really big favor from you," she starts. "This is *huge* and kind of crazy—*really* crazy—but it'd mean so much to me and I hope you'll at least think about it. Well, not that you have a lot of time to think about it, but I still hope you take it seriously, even though it's out there."

I chuckle nervously. "What is it?"

"And as a thank you, I'll do whatever I can to help you out—I could even pull some strings at the office with Susan or Janet if you want to move up higher at the magazine."

"Charlotte, just tell me already."

She sucks in a deep breath. "Promise you won't judge me? Or tell everyone I asked if you say no? It's perfectly okay to say no, too, by the way."

"I promise. Just tell me what it is you want."

She lets out a heavy sigh and blurts, "Can you pretend to be my boyfriend for Christmas?"

DECEMBER 20TH
Charlotte

* * *

Kaden's quiet. So quiet that it feels like minutes, hours, days have gone by where my words just hang in the air.

Can you pretend to be my boyfriend for Christmas?

Ugh, how stupid. It makes me sound desperate. Pathetic. Shallow.

Worse, Kaden probably already has plans for Christmas, even though he said he didn't. It's next week and *everyone* always has at least *something* to do. I texted my ex-boyfriend earlier at the Christmas party, but we broke up over two years ago and he said he's going to his fiancé's house. Luckily, he had the decency not to be too cruel. I'm sure he'll tell everyone about it, though.

Right now, Kaden's just staring at me with his mouth open.

Why hasn't he said anything? I know what I asked is crazy, but he could at least say *something*. Maybe he's trying to decide if I'm serious. Maybe I can play it off as a joke. Maybe that's my escape.

I jump up from the couch and cross my arms in front of the window. "Never mind. Forget it. It's stupid." I wish I had never asked him at all.

"What?" he asks quietly.

"Now that I hear it out loud it just sounds—nope, I take it off the table," I say. "Sorry for wasting your time. If you want to take your food to go when it comes, that's fine. You don't have to eat with me. I understand."

He's quiet again. Why does he do that? He has to know it's killing me. I tuck my shoulders in and shift my weight on my feet. It's all I can do to keep from pacing the room.

He taps his finger against the side of his wine glass. *Tick tick tick.* It's driving me insane.

"Okay, you have to say *something!*"

Kaden smiles. "Come sit down."

I take a seat on the very edge of the couch with my arms still crossed. My leg bounces on the floor. I'm too anxious to relax.

He puts his hand on my knee to steady my leg.

I let out an involuntary smile. "Sorry."

"It's okay." He pulls his hand back and takes a sip of his wine. "Just Christmas Day or Christmas Eve too?"

I swallow to try to alleviate my dry throat. Doesn't work. "Well actually, my parents live on the other side of the state. Near Buffalo. It's an eight- or nine-hour train ride, depending on the day. So it'd be for a full week. We'd have to leave tomorrow morning at nine, too."

"Oh."

My heart begins pounding in my chest. It sounds crazier the more I explain, but is he considering it? Or is taking the full week a deal breaker? I wonder if he would've agreed if we were staying in New York. That would've certainly made everything easier. Might've even eliminated the problem altogether.

"Yeah," I say. "I know, it's too much to ask. I shouldn't have brought it up. Just forget it."

"Well, hold on."

I finally find the courage to ask, "Are you thinking about it?"

He stares down at his glass for a moment. "Maybe. Where would we be staying?"

"With my parents."

"So we'd probably have to stay in the same room then, right?"

I nod. "Probably. They have two guest bedrooms and my sister and her husband are already using one. I could take the floor. I know it'd be really weird for you, but for one week hopefully it won't be too bad."

Silence slips between us again. It's killing me. I don't want to be hopeful, but it doesn't sound like he's completely opposed to the idea, either.

"I'm still confused," he says.

Of course he is. "I'm probably not explaining any of
this very well at all."

"I just don't know why you need to pretend to have a boyfriend at all," he says. "You're beautiful, fun to be around. You have a great job. You live in Manhattan. I assume you have good friends, too."

I let out a deep breath. "Yeah, I do. But none of that seems to matter with my parents. Well, mostly my mom. It's probably just because she doesn't *see* my life firsthand. Whenever I talk to her it's always, 'Have you found a boyfriend yet?' 'Any dates lately?' 'Just you this year?'" My voice jumps an octave into an annoying squeaky voice that sounds nothing like my mother while I imitate her. "I'm tired of it."

He nods. "I could see that."

"And Susan's about to retire and I think I have a really good shot at getting her job. That's been my sole focus in life right now, and I don't think I have time for a boyfriend. But my mom is hellbent on pairing me off. My sister, Olivia, isn't much help, either. She's married with kids. Amy's married with kids. Even though I'm so happy for both of them, I don't think it's what I want right now."

I lean back on the couch and play with my nails. This is too personal to look Kaden right in the eyes, but he needs to know in order to understand my crazy idea. It's also a relief to get this off my chest to someone. And Kaden's a good listener.

"Everyone keeps asking me when I'm going to settle

down," I continue. "They don't really accept the fact that I'm okay being single, you know? So I thought that I could avoid the scrutiny for one year and bring someone home who could pass as my boyfriend and just shut everyone up for a bit."

I rub my face in my hands. I haven't thought much about this scheme and red flags keep jumping out the more it churns in my head.

"Ugh, but it's not like *that's* going to happen. I can't ask you to pop in at every holiday or pose for random pictures throughout the year to keep up this lie that you're my boyfriend. And that's exactly what I'd be doing: lying. I can't do that to my family. They're annoying sometimes, sure, but I don't want to lie to them. That's not fair. They only mean well. And if you show up this time and not next time, it'll probably just make next time worse because I'll be getting the pity looks and the, 'You'll find someone else,' lines and—"

Kaden's laughter pulls me out of myself.

"What?" I ask.

"You're jumping to conclusions now," he says.

I shrug. "Well, you would too if you were in my position."

"Yeah, I guess so," he admits.

I smile at him. "Anyway, thanks for listening. Sorry to bother you with all of this. The food should be here any minute, so you can be on your way then."

He's quiet. *Again.* Does he ever talk?

"What are you thinking?" I ask. "You're not seriously considering this, are you?"

He shrugs.

"It's completely unreasonable!"

"Well yeah, but I *don't* actually have plans for Christmas. Even though I'd be spending the holiday with a bunch of strangers who think that I'm someone that I'm not, it'd probably be better than what I'd be doing here."

Hope bubbles to the surface and I try to shove it down. This idea is too crazy. There's no way he'd agree to it. And if he does, that would make him insane. What kind of psycho would I be bringing home?

"So what are you saying?" I ask.

"As long as you agree to help me at work, I'll help you out next week," he says.

"You will?" I try not to sound too excited, but it doesn't work.

"Yeah. This is kind of insane, but it should make things interesting, at least. Definitely a holiday to remember." He chuckles. "And I *would* like to move up in the publishing world and if you could help me with that in any way, that'd be awesome. Even if you can't, this would make an impressive story." He shrugs again. "Life's an adventure, you know?"

I leap across the couch and hug him, nearly spilling his wine on my pristine couch. I don't care. "Thank you! Thank you! Thank you! Oh, this means so much to me, you have no idea!" I pull away. "I promise, I'll do everything I can to make it up to you. You want a better location for your desk? I'll make it happen. You want a coffee every morning? Done. You want to go for a promotion? Let me write up a recommendation."

He laughs and the doorbell rings. "Well, you could start with getting me some food."

"Done," I say with a smile.

DECEMBER 21ST
Kaden

"Coffee?" I raise the Starbucks cup to Charlotte when she answers the door the next morning in her white bath-robe. I'm standing outside her unit with my suitcase on the floor beside me.

"Thank you!" She takes the cup and steps aside to let me in. "I just need to finish getting ready. Come in and have a seat."

I roll my suitcase inside and leave it by the door.

"You know, I'm supposed to be the one buying you a drink," she says on her way back to her room. "I owe you a lot of them, actually."

"I just figured that since I'm your boyfriend now I should get used to doing chivalrous things." I texted her on my way over to see how she takes her coffee.

"Yeah…" Her voice trails off as she cradles her cup. "I want to thank you again for doing this. You have no idea how much it means to me."

"No problem. Really. It'll be fun being your boyfriend for a week." No lie there.

She gives me a smirk and heads back to her bedroom. "That doesn't start until tonight."

"I'm just getting a head start." I look around for her suitcase but don't find one. "Are you going to be ready on time? It's just after eight."

"I should be fine." Her voice carries from her bedroom. "Our train doesn't leave until nine and it takes a half an hour to get to the station."

"If you say so." I check my watch again. I'm a little anxious.

She closes the door for a few minutes and comes back out in jeans and a tan sweater with a white tank top underneath.

"Wow." The word escapes my lips before I have a chance to stop it.

She smirks. "Still practicing?"

I look down to hide my embarrassment.

Her shoes click against the hardwood floors as she crosses the apartment, grabbing clothes, bags, and other items scattered around the apartment. She carries them back into her room.

"You still haven't packed yet?" I ask.

"It'll only take me a few minutes," she calls to me. "That's something you should know about me—I'm kind of a last-minute person."

"I can see that," I mutter.

"Huh?"

"I said I think we should get to know each other better," I say louder. I look at some of the pictures on the walls. Groups of friends, family pictures from Christmases past, baby pictures—likely of her niece and nephew.

She steps out of the bedroom again with her suitcase trailing behind her. "Yeah, I figured we could talk on the train. I'm all set now, worry-wart."

"Good. How long of a ride is it?"

"Only half an hour to Penn Station." She makes a face. "But eight or nine hours home. Kinda ruins the whole day."

"Sounds like it. Wouldn't it be faster to fly?"

Charlotte reaches for her coat by the door and pulls it on, flicking her hair out from under it. "Faster, sure. Cheaper? Not by a long shot. Besides, do you really want to spend time at an airport the weekend before Christmas?"

I shrug. "Guess not."

"It's insane."

"I've never flown near a holiday, so I'll take your word for it."

She grabs the handle of her suitcase with one hand and the doorknob with the other. "You ready?"

"Yup." I grab my suitcase and step out into the hallway.

She hesitates in the doorway and murmurs, "Lights are off. Stove is off. Blinds are drawn…. I think we're all set."

"Do you have everything you need?" I ask.

"I should." She locks the door behind her. "If I forgot anything, my mom should have it. Do you have everything?"

"Seeing how I'm going into this week kind of blind, I'd say I packed as well as I could."

She cringes and hits the button for the elevator. "Sorry about that."

"It's okay. What about the train tickets. Do you have those?"

"They're on my phone."

"Mine too?"

"Yup. Booked it last night. Another reason why flying wouldn't be the best option. With the train, it doesn't really matter where you sit."

When the elevator arrives, we step in.

"Okay, so right off the bat, here are some things you should know about me," she says once the elevator descends. "I'm not that punctual and I love coffee."

"Two things I've already picked up on."

"Starbucks isn't my favorite, but when you're in New York, you kind of get accustomed to it," she adds. "Well, New York *City*. Where I'm from we have a few more options."

"From your Canadian friends?"

"Yup!"

The elevator dings and we step out onto the sidewalk. Her pace is faster than I expect and much faster than it was last night. Either it's her morning energy or she knows we're short on time.

"Dammit, *that's* what I forgot," she says. "The coffee you brought me is still sitting in my room."

I check the time. "We don't really have time to go back."

"That's okay. I'll just have a mess to clean up when I get back next week."

We meander through the thickening crowd to the subway and hop on the 1 train. Per subway etiquette, we don't say much on the train. It's only a couple stops until we're at Penn Station.

As we follow the signs to the station concourse, I notice the wreaths and garland hanging around many of the support columns throughout the station. They don't do much to dress it up, but I suppose it's better than nothing. Especially when it's busy-as-usual in the growing throng of people. Usually the city's not too busy this early on a Saturday morning, but being the weekend before Christmas and a big traveling day, it's crowded.

When we get inside, we check the departure board for our gate. It's 8:58.

"Track 12 is still boarding!" Charlotte exclaims with a backhand smack to my chest. "Let's go!"

I follow her across the station to the appropriate track.

"Train to Toronto?" the gentleman at the door asks.

"Yup," she says.

"Right this way. Mind your step. Follow the platform until you see another man dressed like me."

"Thank you! Merry Christmas!" Charlotte leads me

down the escalator, bouncing her suitcase on the steps as she descends.

"Toronto?" I ask.

"That's the final stop," she explains. "We're getting off at the first Buffalo stop in Depew. It's one of the final stops on the line, actually."

"Gotcha."

We walk along the platform past several train cars to another man standing by an open door.

"You two are the last ones to board," he says. "Go all the way to the end. There should still be some open seats."

"Thanks," she says breathlessly.

We step inside and spot two free spaces all the way at the other end of the car.

Charlotte lets out a heavy breath of air once we're seated. "See, I told you we'd make it."

Before I have a chance to respond, the train lurches forward.

"Just barely," I add.

"I told you, I'm not that punctual. I try so hard, but it's just not in my blood. Better not to get frustrated about it." She gets her suitcase situated in the space in front of us and pulls her big purse onto her lap. "But I always end up where I need to be."

I settle in and look around. I'm actually doing this. I'm going home with this girl who I barely know. She's nice, sure, but what if her family's crazy? What if she turns out to be crazy? What if this whole week sucks and I can't wait to get back to New York?

Guess I'll have to wait and see.

What's really crazy, though, is that yesterday when I left work I had no intention of going anywhere for the holidays. Now, somehow, I'm going to a place I've never been to before to pretend to be someone I'm not. Although I have pictured myself as Charlotte's boyfriend as recently as two days ago when I asked her out, this is happening faster than I thought it would. Be careful what you wish for, I guess.

As the train rolls through the tunnel out of the city, another train worker comes by with a scanner.

"Get the tickets ready," I tell her.

She continues to fumble in her purse until the man gets to us.

"Tickets," he says.

"Oh!" she says, as if surprised. She pulls up her phone and taps at it. "Just give me one…second. They're in my email somewhere—Oh! Here they are!" She holds her phone so he can scan them.

"All set," he says with a smile. "Enjoy your ride."

"Thank you!" she says, then adds, "Merry Christmas!"

Getting situated in her seat is a whole production for her. Adjusting her suitcase, fixing her purse, taking off her jacket. She fusses until she's finally settled. It makes me laugh to myself, but she doesn't take notice so I don't say anything.

"So, it's probably a good idea that we get to know each

other," she says. "It's a long ride, but we have a lot to cover, too."

"Homework? It's supposed to be my week off."

"You have *no idea* what you've signed up for."

I watch as the train makes its way through the last of the pillars that hold the city up above us. "That's for sure."

"Aha!" She pulls out a pad of paper from her purse and flattens it on her lap. "Here we go."

"You made a list?"

"I told you, there's a lot to cover. Especially since you're going to be around my family twenty-four seven. If they suspect something's up, that'll be embarrassing for both of us—especially me."

"All right, so what do I have to know?"

She looks over the pad of paper—mostly filled with scribbles about who's going to be around, traditions, even some of her favorite foods. "Um…let's start with your family. My folks will want to know why you're not with them and they might not be comfortable asking you outright. So if I explain it to them in private, I would like to give them an honest answer…or pretty close to it. That way we can keep our stories straight."

There goes the fun we've been having so far. "Um…I haven't seen them in a while. But that's not important right now. Your family is who we're going to spend the next week with and it looks like you have a lot to tell me."

She points a manicured finger at me. "True."

"We'll just tell your parents that everyone in my family

was busy this year."

"Okay." She glances at her list and then turns back to me. "So we're going to my mom and dad's house. They still live in Batavia, the town I grew up in, but they bought a different house than where I lived. It has a smaller yard and is within walking distance of everything they need. It's just easier for them to maintain since they're getting a bit older. Plus, to be honest, I think my dad was looking for an excuse to have my mom downsize some of her stuff."

"Did it work?"

"Eh." She shrugs. "In a way, but there's a lot of stuff she just stuck in storage."

"So your dad went from being annoyed by the stuff to having to pay for the stuff."

She smiles. "Now you're getting it! Anyway, that's a big part of my parents' relationship. They complain about each other, but not so much that they're going to break up. I actually think they like the fact that they annoy each other."

I smile. I can imagine. Well, I can imagine from what I've seen on TV.

"Especially at Christmas," she goes on. "Mom likes to go all out and Dad complains about everything she makes him do, but he's usually grumpin' and groanin' as he's climbing up the ladder to put up more lights." She laughs. "This one year, my sister and I caught him laughing to himself up on the roof while my mom was yelling at him from the front door."

"So he does like it."

"I think so."

"Is your sister older or younger?"

"Older, thank God. Could you imagine how pushy my mom would be about me having kids if my *younger* sister is the one who had a family before me?"

"Well, I've never met your mother, but based off of what you said, sure."

"Oh. Right. Well, you'll see this week."

Charlotte's quiet, so I ask, "What are they all going to think of me?"

She considers this. "I'm not really sure. They'll be surprised, definitely. Especially since I haven't mentioned you before, but I think my mom will be really happy. She'll probably treat you like a son-in-law immediately. She usually takes to men better, anyway. I think she's a bit disappointed with me."

"I'm sure that's not true."

"Well, either way, she really wants to see me paired off with someone, like Olivia is."

"What about your dad?" Only once have I met one of my old girlfriends' parents and because they were divorced, I met her step-dad, who wasn't nearly as protective of her as a regular dad would be. At least not in her case. I have no experience in this department and I'm a little fearful.

"He probably won't say much, honestly," Charlotte tells me. "You're new, he doesn't know you. He probably won't say much to you. He'll just keep bickering with my mother."

"And your sister and brother-in-law?"

"Oh, Olivia will love you," she says without hesitation. "You're quiet, sweet, handsome—" She blushes. "You fit the mold of who my sister's always pictured me with.

I grin. "Well, that's a relief."

"And Arthur…well, I honestly don't know him that well," she says. "He's pretty quiet. Whenever we're together, he's usually keeping Madison occupied. I'm sure that'll be even worse now with the new baby, too. Anyway, I think he's a good guy. Olivia seems happy. I just don't really know him."

"Maybe this next week will be your opportunity to get to know him."

She rolls her eyes. "I doubt it, but maybe."

Charlotte dives even further into the details of her family. She tells me about Christmas traditions growing up: taking turns putting up the star, hanging up their handmade Christmas decorations, spending hours in the kitchen baking cookies for the neighborhood. She tells me how she and Olivia used to spend hours outside playing in the snow, getting into snowball fights with other kids on the street.

It's nice to hear about her normal childhood and the traditions that survived despite her family living so far apart now. I wish I had more stories to share with her, but that'll come in time. All I know is that Charlotte's making this a better Christmas than I've had in years and it's only just begun.

December 21st

Charlotte

* * *

I guzzle down half of the water bottle I brought with me. My voice is hoarse from talking so much. I've detailed every pertinent aspect of my life—and even threw in some extra details—and now we're both on our laptops working on Susan's blog posts. I'm reading his posts and he's reading mine.

Kaden's a great writer. His posts are thematic, witty, and very succinct. I should probably take a second look at mine, actually. Hopefully he's adding some of his charm to my posts. I don't have to do much editing to his. It's a relief since I promised him a recommendation.

I finish going through his posts before he's done with mine. After closing up my computer, I lean back against the seat and look across the aisle through the window. The sun is setting and it looks beautiful.

I feel like I've told Kaden all there is to know about me, but there's obviously more to say. It's impossible to *tell* a person who you are over the course of several hours. It's not the best way to get to know someone, but it's better than nothing. It's the only opportunity we've had.

I was worried about how much he retained—the important bits, at least—but when I quizzed him he seemed to remember most of it. And the cover story we came up with is that we've only been dating a month, so they can't expect him to know *everything*. It just might work.

I watch as the sun disappears for moments at a time behind trees and a few buildings. My view shifts down to the couple across the aisle. The man raises their joint hands and kisses hers. It's sweet. It's natural. It's just the sort of thing that couples do.

I hold my hand out to Kaden. "Give me your hand."

He looks at me with surprise. "What?"

I reach over and grab his. It's bigger than I expected. And clammy. I guess I'll have to deal with that.

"What are you doing?" he asks.

I motion with our joint hands across the aisle. "If we're going to pass as a real couple, we need to be comfortable enough to at least hold hands. That comes with practice."

He grins, but doesn't say anything else.

I shift away, but keep our hands locked. "What?"

"Nothing," he says with a shake of his head and that grin still plastered on his face.

"Look, I haven't mentioned you at all before, which

means we have to tell my family that we've only been dating a month, *which means* we'd still be in that annoying honeymoon-hang-all-over-each-other phase. Or at least be somewhat comfortable touching each other—not *touching each other*, but—you know what I mean! It needs to look natural or they're not going to buy it."

"Okay." Again with the grin!

We're still holding hands by time we get to our stop. I let go so we can grab our luggage and get off the train. It's a tiny boxy station that certainly reflects the period it was built in—knowing that is a side effect of working at a home style magazine. There's a black metal fence separating the platform from the parking lot. My parents wave from the other side.

"Hi sweetie!" Mom calls to me with a wave as we step toward the gate. When I get through, she hugs me tight. "Oh, I've missed you so much!"

"I missed you too, Mom."

Dad pulls me in for a hug too and then takes my suitcase from me. "Come on. We'll put this in the car. It's freezing out here."

Mom notices Kaden lingering behind me. Here goes nothing.

I take a step back and reach for his hand. "Mom, Dad, this is my boyfriend, Kaden."

They both stare with eyebrows raised. Now that I'm standing here facing the reality of lying to my parents, I wish I hadn't started this whole thing. What would they say if they ever discovered the truth? Will I be able to keep it a secret from here on out or will it eat at me until I have to reveal it?

It's too late to worry about it now. I just can't let them find out. By Easter, I'll tell them that Kaden and I broke up. Hopefully that'll put this whole thing to rest. For them and my conscience.

Kaden steps forward and extends his free hand, which my father shakes. "Pleased to meet you. I'm Kaden."

Dad gives him a curt nod. "Nice to meet you. I'm Jim and this is my wife Maria."

Mom still looks shocked. She reaches her hand slowly to Kaden and shakes his. "How did this—I wasn't expecting a second person. Charlotte, dear, you never said—" She stops herself and smiles at Kaden. "Well, I guess we'll just have to make room. Come on, let's get out of this cold."

They lead us to Mom's compact SUV parked at the far end of the lot. Dad never likes parking among other cars. We load up our bags and climb in. Dad starts the car and Burl Ives starts crooning through the speakers.

Mom turns down the radio from the passenger seat. "So Kaden, what do you do?" She doesn't like to drive at night and Dad doesn't like her driving. I'm sure they're holding back with their bickering because otherwise Mom would probably be pointing out different things Dad should "watch out" for and he would tell her that she could've driven. They usually go back and forth. Not today, though.

"I'm actually a staff writer at *Home & Hearth*," he says.

"It's where we met," I add quickly. My clammy hand is locked in Kaden's. I can't tell if it's from him or nerves. Probably nerves.

"Oh, how nice!" Mom says. "Now, what's your family up to this Christmas?"

Guess I was wrong about them being too timid to ask.

"*Mom*," I warn.

"What?" she asks innocently.

"Not now," I say quickly. "How are Olivia and the kids?" That'll change the subject.

"Loud," Dad says.

Mom swats at him. "Maddie's just a kid and the baby is just…well, a baby."

"Why do you think I worked so much when you kids were young?" Dad looks at me through the rearview mirror.

She chuckles. "Oh, stop."

The light turns green and the tires spin in the snow as Dad pushes the gas pedal.

"Careful, dear," Mom says.

"I've got it, honey."

Mom watches the road nervously until the car regains traction. She turns back to us and says, "Anyway, Kaden, let us know if there's anything we can do to make your Christmas feel more like home."

He smiles. "I'm sure everything will be fine."

"Well, if something comes up," she says. "If we had

known you were coming, we might've had something extra
prepared."

"Okay, Mom, I get it," I drone. "I'm sorry for springing him on you."

"Oh, stop worrying, dear. It'll be fine."

I look out the window and roll my eyes. I just got here and she's already twisting my words.

"How long have you worked at the magazine, Kaden?" Mom asks.

"Just a couple months."

"And how long have you two been together?"

"About a month," we say in unison.

I suck in my bottom lip and look out the window at all the houses lit up with decorations.

Mom squeals. "Oh, how cute! So I take it that this didn't happen until *after* we last saw you, dear?"

I rock my head back and forth. It needs to be believable and a romance doesn't just pop up out of thin air. It needs time to grow. Time to blossom.

Well, at least with me it does.

"We were talking a bit before then." A deviation from our story, but I think it'll fit in just fine.

"Talking?"

"Flirting, honey," Dad clarifies.

My cheeks flush with embarrassment. Good thing it's dark.

"Oh, I see," Mom says. "Why didn't you say anything? I asked you if you were seeing someone—didn't I ask her, dear?" She turns to my dad.

"Yes, honey, you asked."

"Mom, I'm not going to tell you every time I'm interested in a guy," I say. "There are more important things happening in my life."

She gasps. "Don't say that. I'm sure Kaden's a very big part of your life."

"No, that's not what I meant," I say. "It's just that finding a boyfriend isn't at the top of my priority list."

She waves her hand. "Oh, I know. You're always working so much. Don't get me wrong, we're very proud of you, but isn't it better now that you have someone to *share* it with?"

I don't say anything because I can't give her an honest answer. Kaden's only been my unofficial boyfriend for a little over twenty-four hours now and although I've shared a lot about my life, he still *isn't* my boyfriend. I don't text him all day about how my day is going. I don't vent to him about people who annoy me. I don't rush home to tell him about something exciting that's happened.

I don't have a boyfriend, no matter who's hand I'm currently holding. So no, I can't exactly say one way or another whether things would be better with an *actual* boyfriend.

Mom seems to take the hint and we're quiet. Eventually, she turns up the radio as the Chipmunks sing, "Christmas Don't Be Late." I force myself to stop stewing. I'm not a teenager anymore and it didn't even work then. Fifteen years later it's still not going to solve my problems.

As we get closer to my hometown, I recognize familiar landmarks. The car dealership on the edge of town, "the" roundabout, the old candy store. I smile at the memories.

We meander the tree-lined streets until we're pulling up to my parents' house on East Avenue.

Colored lights line the windows and the frame of the house. Green garland with white lights are wrapped around the posts on the front porch and icicle lights hang along the ceiling of the porch, giving the front door an impressive glow. Dad's even laid lights along the edge of the driveway and front sidewalk that makes the snow glow with an assortment of colors. Through the living room windows, the Christmas tree glistens, revealing even more lights strung up inside.

It might not be the house I grew up in, but it's the house I've spent so many holidays in over the last several years. The fact that it has my parents' personal touch helps, too.

Besides the Christmas lights, the rest of the lights are off in the house when we pull into the driveway.

"Olivia and Arthur must've taken the kids out somewhere," Mom says, as if reading my thoughts.

Kaden helps Dad retrieve our bags from the back of the car and we step into the house from the garage. Before my parents can flick on the lights, the house is already illuminated with so many colored lights running along the edge of the ceiling. Mom's personal flair.

There are a few wrapped gifts under the tree and a few of Maddie's toys are piled in the corner of the small living room—made smaller with the tree. It's a little three-bedroom house, but I like to think of it as cozy. Especially this time of year.

I notice the star is on the tree already. I kind of wish they had waited for me to put it up, but I guess I can't be too disappointed. I *did* come four days before Christmas.

Mom sees me looking at the top of the tree. "Yeah, it was your sister's turn to put up the star and Maddie kept asking why we didn't have one and—"

"It's okay," I say with a smile. "It's just a decoration. We're not kids anymore."

"You'll put it up next year."

"Yeah."

"I was going to put you in the bedroom down here." Mom points down the hall. "The one upstairs is bigger, but with your sister coming with both kids, I gave her that one. I'm not sure this one will be big enough for both of you, though. It's a full-sized bed, but I don't know."

I shake my head. "Don't worry about it. We'll make it work."

Kaden nods. "I'm sure it's fine."

I wonder what he's thinking of these sleeping arrangements. I told him we'd be staying at my parents', but did he expect to share a bed? I wish we had a minute alone to talk about—

"You two should take your things to your room and get settled in," Dad suggests. "Maria, why don't you get dinner started? I'll get them some extra blankets." He looks over at

Kaden. "Sometimes the plastic on those windows doesn't hold up. We've been saving to replace them, but you know how that goes."

Kaden nods politely. "Yeah."

Grabbing my suitcase, I lead my fake-boyfriend down the narrow hallway to the small bedroom at the end. It's obvious this is usually just my parents' computer room. An ancient desktop sits on an oversized desk in the corner. CDs are lined along the shelf above the computer and stacks of papers, discarded gloves, and even some forgotten Christmas lights have piled on top of the desk.

The bed, however, is shoved in the corner, leaving a small walkway to the closet.

"This is—"

"Small," I finish for him as I close the door behind us. I haul my suitcase on top of the bed and pull off my jacket. "I can take the floor, since you're doing me a huge favor."

He shakes his head. "No, I wouldn't feel right about that. I'll just use the extra blankets your dad brings for the floor. You take the bed."

"Are you sure?"

He nods. "Really, it's fine."

"Okay, just remember that it needs to *look* like we've slept together—not *slept* together, but slept...in the same bed, you know?" My face goes red.

He smiles. "I know."

I pull out my clothes and start filling the dresser. "So what do you think so far? Any regrets?"

"I'm in too deep to go back now," he says.

"True. Any comments before we head back out there?"

"It's…different. Nerve-wracking at times. But it beats watching TV all day." He looks around at the pictures on the walls. My sister and I bundled in our snowsuits in the backyard of our old house. Another of the two of us playing with the hose during the summer in that same yard.

"Hopefully it'll get better for you," I tell him. "We'll get a break from my family tomorrow. I'm having lunch with my friend Candace and I figured you'd want to get out of the house too."

"Am I going to get the hometown tour?"

"Would you rather stay home with my parents?"

"I never said I wouldn't come with you."

"Good." I close my empty suitcase and slip it in the closet. "There. I saved room for your stuff too."

"Thanks." He tries to sneak by me in the tight space, but we bump into each other.

There's a knock on the door and we quickly separate as Dad walks in with a couple of heavy blankets.

"Knock knock!" He notices us and pauses, flustered. "Uh, here you go, sweetheart."

I take the stack from him. "Thanks, Dad."

"Your mother said dinner will be ready in about twenty minutes."

I nod. "I'm sure we'll be out there before then."

"Okay. Uh, I'll leave you two to it, then." I can sense

the reluctance within him to close the door again behind him, but he does.

"That was awkward," Kaden says.

"Yeah. My dad can be like that sometimes," I say. "He's just not too thrilled to see his daughter dating someone."

"I bet."

"I guess he did the same thing when Olivia and Arthur got serious."

"Makes sense."

"Yeah." I take a deep breath and say, "I want to thank you again for helping me."

Kaden's still putting his clothes away in the dresser. "It's okay."

"It means a lot to me."

He closes the final drawer and turns to smile at me. "I know. That's why I'm doing it."

That's…not the answer I was expecting. Why would he want to do something nice for me when he doesn't really know me that well?

I clear my throat and try to get my mind off of it. "You know, I was thinking, we might have to, I don't know, *kiss* at some point this week. I know holding hands was weird enough, but if this thing is going to pass off as real, we might want to explore that option."

His face goes redder than Santa's suit and I immediately go into damage control.

"Not that we have to," I add quickly. "If you're not comfortable with that, maybe we should just agree now that

that's where we draw the line."

He nods. "Sure, that'd probably be best for after this is all over. That way there's no weirdness or anything when we go back to just being…whatever."

Whatever. Nothing truer than that definition of our relationship. We weren't exactly friends before this and I'm not sure that we will be after, but for this week he's my boyfriend. Apparently, one that I won't get to kiss.

But he's right. It is probably for the best. That way things can go back to normal—as normal as they can be—after the holiday is over.

"Okay," I say with a heavy breath. "No kissing."

December 21st
Kaden

The stuffing's really good, Mrs. Barlow," I say as I dish out a second helping. I've never had homemade stuffing with sausage in it. I've only had it right out of the box.

"Oh, you're sweet." She reaches for her glass of red wine. "Well, I'm glad you like it. Help yourself to more."

Mr. Barlow cuts into his chicken slathered in gravy. "She uses you kids coming as an excuse to clean the freezer. All I usually get is a TV dinner or macaroni and cheese from the box. And not even the good kind—generic!"

She rolls her eyes. "Would you stop? You act like I deprive you. One look at that tire around your waist says otherwise."

I can tell by the smirks on their faces that they're both enjoying this back-and-forth, just like Charlotte said on the train.

I sit back and take in the atmosphere. It's almost straight out of a movie. Lights and decorations everywhere, two red candles burning in the center of the table, the smell of home-cooked food. It's all very warm and homey. All that's missing is a fire roaring in a fireplace, which they don't even have room for.

"How are you guys doing?" Charlotte asks. "Health-wise?"

"Well, I'm still kicking, despite my mediocre diet," her dad says with a grin.

Mrs. Barlow puts her hand on her husband's arm. A silent warning. "We're fine, dear. In the summer, I take walks each morning and in the winter I'm always out and about with my friends. Your father finds things to keep him busy around here, too."

"There's always something that needs fixing," he adds.

"That's good," Charlotte says. "Do you think you'll get a chance to come out and visit me sometime? My apartment's small, but there's a pull-out couch."

The room goes noticeably quiet. Her father keeps his eyes on his plate and her mother reaches for her wine again.

"We'd love to, dear," her mother starts, "but I can't imagine driving in New York City. And then there's parking and finding someone to watch the house and—"

"Got it," Charlotte says, not meeting their eyes.

"Honey, come on," her dad adds. "It's not that we don't want to see where you live, but it's a long trip and we don't really know the city and—"

"You could take the train," she says. "I'll take a few days off work, meet you at the station, and show you around."

Mrs. Barlow smiles. "That could be nice."

Even I can tell that's just a peace offering.

"So Kaden, where did you grow up?" her dad asks, quickly changing the subject.

"The east end of Long Island. A town called Riverhead."

"Oh, so you're a true New Yorker," he says. "Probably went to the city all the time."

I shrug. "Not really, actually. Besides the tourists every summer, it was actually a lot like this town. Quiet. Safe."

"That's nice," Mrs. Barlow says with a smile.

I can tell Charlotte's still fuming beside me. She scoops up the last of her food and makes to gather her plate, but her mom sits up.

"Oh, I have some cookies I want you all to try." She gets up and moves to the kitchen.

I reach over and squeeze Charlotte's hand. She gives me a hard look that quickly softens when she notices her dad watching. I just wanted her to know that I understand what was going on, but she must just be trying to keep up appearances.

Mrs. Barlow's voice carries from the next room as she works the top off a Tupperware container. "I tried a new recipe using sour cream. It's supposed to give it a unique flavor. Nancy Slater gave it to me. You know, Kimmy and Tracy's mom?"

She's talking to Charlotte, who nods.

"Anyway," she says setting down the container. "Try them and see if you like them. I haven't decided yet, myself. I liked them when Nancy made them, but she must've used a different frosting or something because these don't taste quite the same. Oh, don't worry about having too many. I've already set aside plates for you and your sister to take home with you."

When Charlotte doesn't move, I reach over and grab a cookie. It's delicious, but before I can offer my analysis, the side door opens.

"Hello!" a woman's voice chirps from behind us.

I turn and see a brunette woman stepping in behind a little girl with long blonde hair. She can't be any older than three or four. A man follows, holding a baby carrier.

Charlotte's face lights up and she rushes over to them. She kneels in front of the girl and smiles wide. "Hi, Maddie! Can I have a hug?"

The girl looks up at her mother, unsure.

"Give Aunt Char a big hug," she says.

The girl steps forward and Charlotte scoops her up and squeezes her tight. "Don't you remember me from your birthday party?"

The girl squirms until she's back on her feet.

I notice Charlotte's smile falter, but she recovers when her sister steps forward for her own hug.

"She's tired," she says against Charlotte's shoulder. "How have you been? I've missed you so much!"

They pull away and Charlotte responds, "I'm good.

Work's busy, as usual. What about you?"

"Full-on mom duty now that Baby Ken is here."

"Oh, I can imagine. Can I see him?"

The man sets the carrier on the floor. "He just fell asleep in the car. I think I might take him upstairs and put him to bed. It's a late night for such a little guy." He smiles up at Charlotte. "Nice to see you again."

"You too." She returns the smile quickly, but kneels down to see the sleeping baby wrapped in layers of warmth. "Oh! He's so adorable! Look at those cheeks!"

Her sister smiles. "He's got chipmunk cheeks, that's for sure." She turns to her husband. "You should probably put him to bed before he wakes up." She looks over at her yawning daughter. "You too, sweetie."

"No!" she whines.

"Yes," the woman nods. "Go on, Daddy will tuck you in."

The man reaches for her hand and lifts the baby carrier with the other. "Come on. Say good night."

They stalk off toward the staircase at the end of the hallway.

When he's gone, Mrs. Barlow clears her throat and announces proudly, "Charlotte brought a guest."

"Oh!" The woman offers her hand to me. "I wasn't even paying attention. Sorry about that. I'm Olivia, Charlotte's sister."

I stand and shake her hand. "Kaden, Charlotte's, uh, boyfriend."

She smirks at Charlotte and then turns back to me. "Come on, we need to talk." She puts her arm around my shoulder and leads me to the small living room at the front of the house.

Behind me, I hear Mrs. Barlow ask Charlotte to help with the dishes. Guess I'm on my own with this one. Especially because Mr. Barlow follows us to the living room, too.

"So, Kaden, is it? Where are you from?" Olivia asks once we've taken our seats.

"Long Island," her father says as he clicks on the TV. "Riverton or River City or something."

I smile. "Riverhead."

"That's it!" He waves his hand at me and kicks his feet up on the recliner.

"How'd you meet my sister?" Olivia asks.

"I work with her."

"At the magazine?"

"Yeah."

She fixes her hair and nods, likely buying time to think of more questions. "Interesting, interesting."

I chuckle. "Okay, immediately, I hate that."

She smiles. "Just trying to determine if you're a good match for my sister."

"She's trying to decide if she likes you," Mr. Barlow corrects.

"Dad!" she scolds, then turns back to me. "Do you smoke?"

"No."

"Drink?"

"Not really. Not often, at least."

"I'm going to guess that you work out a bit."

I smirk. "Yes. Not to mention, I live in the city. We walk everywhere."

"True. How long have you lived there?"

"Well, I first moved there when I went to NYU and I never moved away."

"Where'd you take Charlotte on your first date?"

I hesitate. We hadn't discussed this. Quickly, I try to come up with something sweet but still kind of generic in case Charlotte is telling her mom a different version of the same story.

"Dinner and a movie. We walked around a bit afterward. Talked, got to know each other, you know?" That was originally my intention for tonight when I asked Charlotte out a few days ago. Somehow I ended up coming home to meet her family instead. All before we had a proper date, which is unlikely to happen at this point.

"Did you kiss her?"

"Olivia, come on," Mr. Barlow says. "Let the man breathe!"

She narrows her eyes and looks at me, waiting for an answer. What's better? Kissing her right away or waiting until Date #2?

"Yes," I say. "On the cheek."

"Okay," she says with a nod. "You have my preliminary

approval. I'll make my final decision after a brief observation period."

I laugh. "Okay, good."

The man comes back downstairs—what was his name? Charlotte told me on the train, but she told me so much, it's hard to keep it all straight. Maybe if I wait long enough, someone else will bring it up. Then again, this is the first time Boyfriend Kaden is meeting any of these people. Names are not something he should be expected to remember.

"Well, the kids are finally asleep again." He places a baby monitor on the coffee table and takes a seat on the other end of the couch. "Baby Ken wasn't happy when I pulled him out of the carrier, but he settled down."

"That's good," Olivia says. She motions between me and the man. "Kaden, this is my husband, Arthur. This is Charlotte's boyfriend."

Arthur! That's his name! We reach across the couch and shake hands.

"Arthur's a nutritionist at one of the hospitals in Columbus, Ohio, so we live out there," she explains.

I nod. "Yeah, Charlotte told me." *That* I remember. "That sounds like a cool job."

He shrugs. "It can be. Some days it's a job, just like any other, you know?"

"Oh yeah," I say with a chuckle. "I'm a staff writer at the same magazine Charlotte works at and sometimes they assign me a story that I *really* don't care to write about."

"What's the worst thing you've written about?" Olivia asks.

I consider it. "Um…probably bathroom handle nobs, but I don't really care for anything with gardening, either."

"Bathroom nobs?" Arthur asks. "What kind of magazine is it?"

"It's called *Home & Hearth*. It's like HGTV, but on paper."

They both nod. "Gotcha."

"You ever do anything on weed killers?" Charlotte's dad asks.

"I don't really know," I admit. "I've only worked there a few months."

"Oh, well in the summer, we get those weeds coming up between the sidewalks—"

"Dad, he said he doesn't like gardening stuff," Olivia says.

"Just listen," he pushes. "We get those weeds coming up between the cracks, you know? I've sprayed them with—" He raises his voice to shout into the kitchen. "What's that weed sprayer we used, honey?"

"What?" she calls back.

"That weed sprayer!" he shouts louder. "The one we used on the sidewalk!"

"The CD player?"

He waves his hand in her direction. "Anyway, we sprayed it with a couple different things and they keep coming back. I just wanted to know if you knew of any-thing, that's all."

"Have you tried pulling them?" Arthur suggests.

"I have to! Nothing else works!"

"Dad, he's not a gardening expert," Olivia says.

"Can't I just ask a question?"

"No, I don't think we've done anything like that," I say with a polite smile. "You might be better off asking Char-lotte."

"Does she garden out there?" he asks, hopeful.

I falter. "Uh…no, I don't think so. I'm just saying, she's worked at the magazine longer. She might've already done research on this for a story."

"Oh." He nods. "That's a good idea."

The rest of the evening goes on more or less the same. We watch the old claymation specials and occasionally Ol-ivia or Arthur will throw out a question my way. Nothing too personal, just random details. Do I live in Manhattan? Too expensive. Do I cook? Only when I have to. Do I have any pets? Can't in my apartment.

Charlotte and her mother join us once they're done in the kitchen, but there's a noticeable shift in the room when they do. I wonder if it has anything to do with her parents not wanting to come to New York to see her apartment. Or maybe me. Or both.

Later, after we've all decided to go to bed, I quickly change into a pair of pajama pants and an old T-shirt to sleep in while Charlotte changes in the bathroom. When she comes back in, she pulls out her laptop.

"All right, let's get these blog posts uploaded before we forget." She sits cross-legged on the bed.

I take a seat on the extra blankets on the floor I laid out for my bed. "So I take it my writing was adequate?"

She glances up at me over the computer screen. "They were great."

I smile, knowing that she begrudgingly admitted I have talent. "Like *great* great or just great?"

A heavy sigh. "They're quick blog posts, Kaden. They're not going to win you any Pulitzers."

Apparently, she's not in the mood. "Oh. Okay."

It's quiet while she clicks around, uploading each story.

"Sorry," she finally says. "Your articles were really good."

"You sound surprised." She's one of the editors, so I always thought she knew my skill level.

"I guess I've never really noticed before," she says. "When you're proofing the magazine, I don't really pay attention to bylines. I'm looking more at grammar and sentence structure."

"Gotcha."

"Yeah. This should only take me a minute."

I lay back in my makeshift bed and wait for her to finish up. I scroll through my phone a bit, but nothing too interesting is on there. Same old stuff, like always. I put away my phone and look around the room. Now that the day is over, reality has set in. I'm really here, pretending to be Charlotte's boyfriend for the week. Her family seems nice enough, but they're not my family. Good thing I have experience being the odd man out in situations like this. I've gotten through awkward moments before, I can get through this week.

Finally, ten minutes later, she closes up her laptop and sets it on the nightstand. "Are you sure you're going to be comfortable?" She lays back and crawls underneath the covers. "We could switch if you want."

I shake my head. "No, this will be fine."

"If you say so. Do you have enough blankets to keep warm?"

"I think I'll be okay."

"Wake me up if you're cold." She lays back and plays on her phone for a little bit.

"You can turn out the light whenever you're ready," I tell her.

No response.

"Charlotte?"

She lets out a heavy sigh. "My family's annoying."

I let out a quick laugh. Guess she's not quite ready for bed. "It's only been a few hours. Your sister and brother-in-law seem nice. Your dad's kind of quirky, but that's okay."

"Yeah," she says with another sigh. "The biggest problem is my mom."

"Not wanting to come visit you?"

"Well yeah, but it's not just that. I mean, it's annoying that they visit Olivia all the time and that's a farther drive for them. But my sister has a house and she has the kids and her life is *normal.*"

"Your life is normal too," I say.

"But not the 'normal' my mom wants it to be," she says. "I don't have a backyard. I don't have a car. Up until today, I didn't have a partner."

"She just wants to make sure you're doing okay. Having a tiny apartment and no backyard might seem like a depravation of sorts to her. She just wants you to have the same things as she does."

"I know, but she needs to back off." She rolls over on the edge of the bed and looks down at me. "Do you know what she asked me while we were doing the dishes?"

"What?"

"She wanted to know if you and I had talked about marriage yet—we told her we've only been dating a month!"

"Shh," I warn.

She drops her voice, but not the exasperation. "She's completely insane about this and it's pushing me away. It's probably why I felt the need to lie to her about having a boyfriend. I don't like keeping secrets from my family, but I just feel so…disconnected sometimes."

"I could see that," I say. "But don't you think you should tell them all of this?"

"And then what? Have them tell me I'm overreacting or make some empty promise to come see me? My mother's not going to be happy until I'm married and living in a house. That's that."

I don't know what else to say, so I don't say anything. These are all genuine issues that she has and I don't know where exactly I fit into this. Should I just listen like a friend? Offer a solution like a boyfriend? Ignore it like the acquaintance that I am?

"And Maddie doesn't even remember me," she says in a quiet voice. "She's going to grow up not even knowing her aunt and it sucks because I love her so much."

"I know, but it's just because she doesn't know you," I say. "Her memory isn't as long as yours. The people she cares most about right now aren't the ones who send her money for her birthday but the ones who play barbies with her or makes her laugh. Use this week to do that and the next time you see her, do the same thing. She'll remember you more and more. It just takes time."

"Yeah, I guess you're right."

"By the end of next week, she'll give her Aunt Char a big hug goodbye."

"Hopefully." She smiles at me. "Thanks for listening. You ready to go to sleep?"

"Yeah, that's fine."

She reaches over and clicks off the light.

DECEMBER 22ND
Charlotte

❄ ❄ ❄

*H*ere, you can play with this one." Maddie hands me one of her Barbies in a yellow floral dress and only one white heel.

"What's her name?" I ask. We're sitting on the floor in the living room.

"That's Julie, she's a mommy."

"Oh yeah? What about yours? What's her name?"

Maddie looks at her doll, dressed in a long black dress. "This is Miss Cooper."

"Miss Cooper, huh? So formal. Is she a mommy too?"

"Nope." She shakes her head. "She's a boss."

I throw my head back and laugh. "I'm sure she is."

Olivia suggested I play with Maddie while I wait for Kaden to get out of the shower. Arthur's watching TV with my dad and Mom and Olivia are making something that smells delicious in the kitchen. The sweet scent of chocolate wafts into the living room.

Maddie and I pretend her doll is going to work while mine stays home and does "mommy things." She uses a shoebox my mom pulled out from the closet as a makeshift dollhouse. She tells me where the imaginary rooms are in the box and lets me know when I'm referring to something wrong.

"No, *that's* the potty, not the kitchen!"

She's certainly got an imagination.

Kaden comes out with his hair still damp and smelling good. He kneels down next to us with a smile on his face.

"You ready to go?"

Maddie puts up her hand. "Hold on. Miss Cooper is on her way home from work and Julie *just* put dinner on the table."

He laughs. "Oh, okay then. Do you think I could steal Aunt Char once Miss Cooper gets home?"

"I can play with you later today," I tell her.

She sighs and rolls her eyes dramatically. "Fine."

Arthur takes my place on the floor when I get up. "Come on, Mads, I'll play with you. Can I be Miss Cooper?"

"No," Maddie says firmly. "She's an independent woman."

I'm still smiling as I put on my coat by the door.

"Where are you two off to again?" Mom comes out of

the kitchen with a messy apron hanging from around her neck.

"We're having lunch with Candace." I button up my coat. "I asked to borrow your car, remember?"

"Oh yeah, that's right. Tell her I say hello and congratulations."

"Will do." Candace and her husband just had a baby a couple months ago. I wonder if the baby will be there too.

Out in the garage, we get into my mom's car and I push the button for the overhead door.

"We can't walk there?" Kaden asks.

"It's a bit of a hike in the cold," I explain. "In the summer, it'd be perfect."

"Gotcha. Does Candace know the truth about us or should we act like we're together here too?"

"Uh…" I hadn't considered only pretending in front of my family, but I can't risk it. It's such a small town that word could spread quickly. "It's probably best to stick to our story."

"Okay."

I back out of the driveway and head toward the center of town. Luckily, there's street parking so we don't have a long walk to the door. It's the brewery and restaurant on Main Street. It's got a nice vintage feel that reminds me of one of my favorite restaurants back in New York. Except, this place is roomier.

Candace and Jamie are already seated at a hightop table in the center of the room and we make our way over there.

"Charlotte!" Candace jumps up and gives me a hug. "It's so good to see you! You look fantastic!"

I pull away and look her over. "Oh my gosh, so do you! I can't even tell you just had a baby."

She pulls her sweater closed. "Oh, you're just being nice. I still have a few more pounds to lose."

"I'm sure you'll get there," I say. "I wouldn't worry too much about it." I look over at her husband and wave. "Hi, Jamie."

They've only been married a little bit. I remember coming home to be one of Candace's bridesmaids. I think I was a fill-in for Tracy Slater, but I'm sure that was only because she wanted to match the number of people on Jamie's side. Social politics during weddings are a nightmare.

It isn't until after we take a seat that I remember I should be introducing Kaden.

"Oh! This is Kaden." Short and sweet. No need to define our relationship. Let them assume whatever they want to assume. I know I told Kaden to make it seem like we're together, but Candace is one of my good friends. She might be able to see right through that.

Both Candace and Jamie shake hands with him.

"Nice to meet you both," Kaden says with a polite smile.

"So how's the baby?" I ask to divert the conversation away from my fictional relationship.

"He's great," Candace gushes. "It's so awesome."

"Especially now that he's sleeping through the night," Jamie adds.

I chuckle. "I'm sure that helps. I thought you'd bring him."

"No, we left him with Jamie's mom," she explains. "I wanted to catch up with you because I haven't seen you since last Christmas and I didn't know how long we'd talk for."

"We have a couple kids back at the house anyway," Kaden says.

I think he means it as a joke, but it thoroughly confuses Candace and Jamie.

"You have kids?" Jamie asks.

I wave it off. "No, my sister's kids. We're all staying with my parents this week."

"Oh, that sounds…" Candace keeps a halfhearted smile.

"It's not that bad, but I am glad to spend some time away from them," I say.

"How are your parents doing?" Candace asks.

"Good. Mom's in heaven this week with the kids around."

"Maddie's a real riot, too," Kaden adds.

"How old is she?" Jamie asks.

Kaden turns to me with his forehead scrunched. "What is she? Four?"

I nod. "Yup, going on sixteen."

Candace laughs. "We won't have to worry about that for a little bit, won't we, honey?" She looks to her husband. "Although if he's anything like you, he's going to be a handful."

He feigns surprise. "What are you talking about? I was

a perfect angel."

"Mm-hmm." She can't contain her smile as she looks at him. It's nice that they care so much for each other. I doubt Kaden and I have that sort of connection. It takes years and a certain level of comfort to develop that. They probably see right through our supposed union.

"So Kaden, what do you do?" Jamie asks.

"I'm a staff writer at the same magazine Charlotte works at," he says.

"That's cool," Jamie replies.

"Do you guys ever do stories on big-name people?" Candace asks. "Or is it all just design and style and stuff?"

"Well, it's *mostly* home design, but there's also recipes in each issue and we usually do an interview with a designer or architect or someone professional like that," I explain. "We don't really have the budget to do the big-name stories."

Candace blushes. "Oh. Guess that shows how much I read the magazine."

I smile. "Thanks for your support!"

"Well, I think it's awesome that you're doing so well," she says. "I'm very proud of you. I'm just being a mom for a bit."

"That's a lot of work," I say.

She lets out a deep breath. "Yeah, it is. I love it, but sometimes I look at people from high school who are hugely successful and I get a bit jealous."

Jamie reaches for her hand.

"Well, nobody's going to match Tracy's success," I say. "And it's not like you're not successful. What you deem as success is different than everyone else, you know? You're starting a family, which is important to you."

Tracy Slater is one of the biggest success stories to come out of this little town. She was Candace's best friend in high school. They both performed in plays and musicals together, only Tracy has gone on to be a huge pop star while Candace chose a more private life.

"Yeah, I know. And I'm very happy to have my family, but it's not traveling the world."

"Yeah, I guess that's true. Have you heard from Tracy lately?"

Candace nods. "She's in town again. Her and Steve have a house here and I guess they're off for the holidays."

"Yeah, I saw how that all went down this past year. I'm glad she's kind of taking control of it, though."

Tracy divorced her husband last year after a domestic violence incident. Several months ago, she married her high school boyfriend and is taking full advantage of the publicity that surrounded her personal life by funneling it into new music. So it seems she's back on top.

"Me too," Candace says. "She's been so busy that I haven't kept up with her as much as I wanted to."

"You've also been busy with the baby."

"She offered to fly us out to her show in Atlanta in April," Jamie says.

"Yeah, and I was six months pregnant."

"Wait," Kaden interrupts. "Are you talking about Tracy *Slater*?"

I smile at his fascination. "Yeah, she went to school with us."

"I didn't know she was from here!" He gushes. "That's so cool!"

"Anyway, if she's back in town you should try to meet up with her," I suggest to Candace.

She nods. "Yeah, we're hanging out the day after Christmas. She says she has a lot to tell me."

"I'm sure she does."

The conversation shifts to other people from high school. People who are still in town, some happy, others not. It makes me a bit nostalgic to be reminded so much of the place I grew up. Although it's hard to ignore the fact that so many people from high school have families now. There's really no escaping it.

After nearly two hours, I check the time. "Ugh, we should probably head back. My mom wants the whole family to come with her to drop off cookies to the neighbors."

"She still does that?" Candace asks.

"Oh yeah. I'm surprised she didn't send me with a plate for you guys."

Jamie holds up his hands. "We have enough junk food at home."

"His mom likes to bake, too." She checks the time on her phone. "We should probably get going also. I'm sure

Jamie's mom is ready to relieve her baby duties."

He laughs. "My mother? *Grandma*!? I wouldn't be so sure."

"I'm going to run to the bathroom before we go," I tell Kaden.

"I'll go with you." Candace jumps from her seat and follows me to the ladies' room. "So Kaden's nice."

"Yeah, he's great." I check my face in the mirror, sensing a longer conversation that I'd rather not have between the stalls.

"Is he…?"

"Is he what?"

"You know, are you two boyfriend-girlfriend?"

I roll my eyes with a smirk. "This isn't high school, Candace. Yes, we're together."

"But is it *official*? That's what I'm asking."

I consider telling her the truth, but the fact that I don't live here anymore might spread the gossip. People might feel like they can talk freely because the chances of me hearing about it are slimmer. But my family might still hear about it.

Better to be vague.

"I don't know," I say, trying to tiptoe around a lie. "It's still new."

"If I were you," she says, "I'd make sure to lock him down real quick."

I don't say anything. Only smile. She's right. Kaden's great, but this is all just an elaborate fantasy. He's not my boyfriend. And by creating a false history, I'm not sure he ever will be.

That idea makes me sadder than I thought it would.

December 23rd

THE LIVING ROOM *is a mess. Ripped and crinkled wrapping paper litter the room. Mom and Dad are buried on the couch together under their new gifts. Maddie leans against Mom's legs and plays with her new Barbie while baby Ken plays with the paper. Arthur reads the box from his back massager in the recliner in the corner and Kaden sits beside me with his hand interlocked with mine.*

"I think that's everything," Olivia says from the floor by the tree. "There's nothing left."

"Wait, not everyone gave their gifts," Mom says. "Olivia, you got me the bathrobe and your father got me the kettle. Charlotte, dear, where are your presents?"

I sit up in bed with a jolt. How could I forget the presents? Am I really that self-absorbed that I thought I'd go home for *Christmas* without bringing any gifts for my family? I'm a horrible person.

"What's the matter? What time is it?" Kaden asks in a groggy voice from the floor. My sudden movement must've woken him. The sun has just started to peek through the blinds.

"I forgot the presents."

"In New York?" he asks with a yawn. "So send them when we get back." He rolls over.

I reach down and shake him. "No, I never *bought* any. Kaden, Maddie's going to hate me if I don't get her anything for Christmas. And I can only imagine the drama that will ensue when Mom realizes I never got anyone anything."

He rolls over and looks at me through slits in his eyelids. "She's not going to hate you and your mother just needs to chill."

"Kaden, imagine if you woke up on Christmas without any gifts?"

"She'll get gifts."

"That's not the point. I want them to have something to open."

"So we'll go shopping sometime."

I lay back. Yeah, there's still two days until Christmas. I have time. Not much, but I can work with it.

I lean over the edge again. "What about wrapping? I need to do that."

"So pay for gift wrapping."

"But then it'll look like I forgot."

He covers his eyes with his hands. "So we'll pick up some wrapping paper and wrap them before we come back. How's that sound?"

Slowly, I lean back again. "Yeah, maybe that'll work."

Getting out of the house and away from everyone

else will give my mother less of a chance to figure out that Kaden's not my boyfriend.

"WHAT ARE YOU two up to today?" Mom asks as she clears the plates from breakfast. She normally doesn't make anything in the morning, but she's probably making an exception because everyone's home. Plus, it's probably her way of trying to get us all to spend the day together. Not that it worked since everyone except for the three of us has already left.

"I was hoping we could borrow the car to run some errands." I gather up the glasses and carry them into the kitchen. Kaden follows behind with the syrup we used on our pancakes.

"Well, your father is out getting firewood with your Uncle Paul and Olivia, Arthur, and the kids are getting ready to go to that Christmas fair thing in Hamburg," Mom says as she rinses off the dishes. "I was *planning* on stopping over at Nancy Slater's house to play cards, but if you don't mind dropping me off I suppose you could take it."

I smile wide. "Fantastic! Thank you!"

"You do remember how to drive, right?"

I roll my eyes with a grin. "I drive in New York sometimes."

"*You do?*"

"Yeah, if I need to, I rent a car. It's not that bad."

She raises her eyebrows so high they're practically touching the ceiling. "Charlotte, those drivers are crazy!"

"It's not a big deal, Mom," I say quickly. "Anyway, thanks for letting us take the car. I promise we'll fill it up when we bring it back."

"I'll see if Nancy can give me a ride home, so take your time getting back."

"How long do you think the house will be empty for?"

Again, her eyebrows go up. "Charlotte Ann, if you think just because you bring a boyfriend home that you two can—"

"Mom. Mom! *Mom!*" I repeat over her to try to stop her. I close my eyes and cringe when she finally stops. I can only imagine what Kaden's thinking. "That's not what— we're not going to—*no*, Mom."

Kaden laughs. "Charlotte's just wondering if we're going to have a family meal again tonight or if we're on our own for dinner."

"Oh." Mom's face lights up. "Well, I think a family dinner would be lovely. I'll text everyone and let them know. In the meantime, I should get ready to go."

When she's gone, I turn to Kaden and smile. "That was a nice save."

He shrugs. "Well, I really enjoyed the family dinners the past two nights. I thought it might be nice to do it again."

I nod. "Maybe, yeah." I shuffle back to our room to finish getting ready for the day, but Kaden wanting another family dinner is still on my mind. I wonder what world he comes from where family dinners aren't the norm. I know there are a lot of families that don't sit down to meals like mine does, but I figured Kaden's family always did. Whoever they are. Maybe he needs this family Christmas just as much as I do.

"WHAT TIME DO you think you'll be home, dear?" Mom holds the back door of her car open, letting the heat escape the vehicle. We're sitting in Mrs. Slater's driveway.

"Oh, before you, I'm sure. We won't be gone long."

"Well, don't rush yourself," she says. "But do plan on dinner at six. I'll make that casserole that's been sitting in the freezer since Thanksgiving."

"Sounds good," I say, rubbing my gloved hands together.

She pauses, muttering to herself, "I have a ride home… Dinner at six… Is there anything else…" Finally, she says, "Nope! That's it. Have fun, you two." She slides out of the seat and closes the door.

"She likes to linger, doesn't she?" Kaden asks.

"Oh yeah." I back out onto Ellicott Avenue and head toward Richmond. "She always wants to make sure she's said everything she wanted to say, so she sits and thinks about it before leaving. Doesn't matter if it's in the house, the car, the middle of the grocery store, whatever. She always pauses."

He laughs. "Sounds like you."

"Does not!"

He gives me a look, but I still don't admit that I've noticed the similarities too.

We're quiet as I pull onto I-90 and head west. I don't break the silence until I've merged into traffic.

"So I figured we'd just go to the mall today and see if we could find something for everyone."

"Do you have any ideas?" he asks.

I rock my head back and forth. "A few. I know my sister in and out, so she shouldn't be a problem. And I can also get her and Arthur a joint gift, so he'll be covered too. Maddie will be relatively easy and so will baby Ken. My dad could probably use something for outside and my mom…I don't know."

"Well, hopefully you'll find something," he says.

"Yeah."

"So what should I expect for this week?" he asks. "Is there more family coming? Is it on Christmas Eve *and* Christmas Day or just one or the other? How many more people am I going to meet?"

How many more people am I going to lie to is what I hear.

This whole thing has ballooned to be more than I thought it would. I didn't expect my extended family to meet him. Guess it shows how little thought I put into this.

"Well, my aunts and uncles come on Christmas Eve—my mom's sisters. They're even more critical than my mother, so I'll have to do my best to keep them away from you."

"Yes, please," he says with a chuckle.

"Sometimes my cousins come too with their spouses, but they've been busy the past couple years, so I'm not sure they'll be there. But my aunts are the ones you have to worry about."

"I'm sure it'll be fine."

"What if they ask how long we've been dating?" I ask.

"A month."

"First date?"

"I told your sister it was dinner, a movie, and a stroll around town. Kiss on the cheek at the end."

"That works. Marriage?"

"Hasn't been brought up yet."

"Kids? Sex?"

"Charlotte, you're overreacting."

I let out a breath of air and grip the steering wheel. "I hope you're right."

By the time we get to the mall, it's crowded, which I should've expected. I manage to find a parking spot at the end of the lot and when we get inside, we're chilled to the bone.

"The winters are a little intense up here," I say to Kaden.

"And it's only the second official day of winter."

"Which means it's only going to get colder."

We start off at my sister's favorite department store and I find her a nice sweater within a few minutes. Easy enough. We stop at one of the kiosks in the concourse and pick up a restaurant gift card for her and Arthur. One of the chain restaurants. Something they can use back in Columbus.

I look in the kitchen store but can't find anything for my mother. She has everything she needs, I think. In my dream she got a big pot, but I don't know if she really needs one.

"What about getting her one of those ready-made baking kits?" Kaden suggests.

I make a face. "She likes to bake from scratch."

He points across to the Lindt store. "Chocolate's always a good option."

"Yeah," I say heavily. "I just want to get her something with substance, you know?"

"Pictures?"

"I thought of that, but we don't have any recent pictures of us." I lead him back out into the concourse. "The last picture we took together—that we actually look good in—was from my cousin's wedding a couple years ago. That won't work."

"We'll just have to keep looking."

"What about you?" I ask. "Is there anything you need to pick up for your family?"

He looks out into the sea of people. "No, I'm fine."

"Are you sure?" I shift the shopping bag to my opposite

hand. "I feel bad that I've taken over your holiday week."

"I told you, it's not a big deal. Where are we headed to next?"

I point to the end of the concourse at another large department store. "I should be able to find a few toys for the kids, something outdoorsy for my dad, and maybe even something for my mom. Maybe."

He stops and hooks his thumb over his shoulder. "Well, it sounds like you've got most of it figured out. I'm going to stop at the food court and get something to drink. Text me when you're ready."

"Oh. Okay. I'll try to hurry."

I feel a twinge of sadness as he turns and walks away in the opposite direction. I was kind of looking forward to spending the day with him. But then, I'm shopping for people he doesn't really know. This is probably an incredibly boring day and this whole week is already due to my selfishness. He's being such a good sport through it, though.

As I continue to the next store, I realize that there's a good chance Kaden might not open anything on Christmas. I was so determined to make sure my family had something that I completely forgot about the person who's doing me the biggest favor this year.

I pull out my phone and text Kaden. *This place is mobbed. Take your time, it might take me a while.*

The store actually doesn't have that many people in it, considering it's two days before Christmas, but I want to buy time to look around for something for Kaden. I owe

it to him and he deserves it. I don't know very many other
guys who'd put up with my family voluntarily. I certainly
didn't even want to. Kaden's special.

DECEMBER 23RD
Kaden

❄ ❄ ❄

Charlotte plops her shopping bags on top of the bed when we get back to her parents' house. We're the only ones home and it gives us the perfect opportunity to make sure everything is wrapped and stowed away so no one discovers that Charlotte forgot to buy everyone gifts.

"You stand guard while I go look for the wrapping paper," she says. "Just in case they come home early."

I give her a mock-salute. When she's gone, I push the blankets thrown on the bed out of the way and clear more space in the small walkway that's become my own resting place each night. In the kitchen, I search through the drawers until I find a pair of scissors and some tape. By time I return to the bedroom, Charlotte's setting down a long tote filled with rolls of wrapping paper.

"My mom likes to be prepared," she says, a little breath-less. "She has another one just like this in the basement."

"I can see that!" I reach down and grab a roll with green wreaths on a crimson red background. "Where do you want me to start?"

She takes the roll from me. "You don't have to do this. It's my own fault we spent the day shopping. I feel bad enough as it is about that."

I reach for the roll again, but she keeps a firm grip. "I don't mind."

"Kaden."

"Charlotte."

"Come on, I need to get this done before everyone comes home."

"Wouldn't it go faster if you stopped arguing with me and just let me help?"

She sighs and lets go of the roll. "Fine. Are you any good?"

I pop the paper on the top of her head. "You'll just have to wait and see."

That makes her smile. She climbs on the bed and cross-es her legs, sorting through the gifts. "All right, let's see what we've got here." She hands me a package. "Here, these are for my dad. See if you can find a box or something to put them in."

"Wouldn't a gift bag be easier?" I ask.

She hooks an eyebrow. "And where's the fun in opening that? My father's been through a lot in his life, I think he deserves to enjoy the happy anticipation that comes with ripping off the wrapping paper from a box. Besides, if you think I'm going to lower my gift-wrapping standards to allow gift bags for everything, you're crazy."

"Sheesh, I didn't realize you felt so strongly about something you forgot about until this morning."

She smiles. "Touché."

I dig through Mrs. Barlow's tote filled with wrapping paper, gift bags, tags, and other related items to find a flattened box. By time I retake my seat against the wall, Mariah Carey is soulfully singing, *"I-I-I don't want a lot for Christmas..."* from Charlotte's phone.

She snatches up a roll from the tote and gets to work on wrapping up her sister's sweater on the bed.

"This used to be one of my favorite parts of the season," she says. "Putting on some music, wrapping up everyone's gifts, trying to make each special so they have a big smile on their face when they open it."

"It's not anymore?" I ask.

She shrugs and takes the tape I set on the nightstand. "It just seems more like a chore now. My life is always so *go-go-go* that it hasn't really even set in that Christmas is in two days."

"You just have to make your own fun."

"Oh yeah? You're not exactly Mr. Holly-Jolly over there."

"Nor am I the Grinch, either."

"True." She runs the scissors along the paper, expertly

cutting it without having to clamp them down. "So what were some of your Christmas traditions growing up?"

I shrug. "The same as everyone else's, I guess."

She rolls her eyes. "Kaden, now that you're my boyfriend you're going to need to give me more than that."

I give her a smile. "I'm planning on breaking up with you at the end of the week."

"Not if I break up with you first." Before I offer my retort, she adds, "Come on! I've told you so much about me and you haven't said much about you. I know I can be a self-absorbed person, but I'd like to at least know if I'm sharing a room with a serial killer or not."

The song ends with the happy chorus fading out. In the silence before the next one begins, I decide it wouldn't be the end of the world to divulge in my history a little bit. After all, she *has* shared so much of hers.

"Okay, so my Christmases *weren't* like everyone else's," I start. "Not really, anyway. My parents both died in a car accident when I was five and I grew up in foster homes."

I watch as the smile on her face quickly slides into a frown.

"That must've been horrible," she says.

I shrug. "None of the families I was with were too terrible. Some were stricter than others. Some were *cleaner* than others, but for the most part, it wasn't the worst childhood."

"But it wasn't with your parents."

I smooth out a piece of tape on the back of the box to

avoid meeting her sad expression. "No, it wasn't."

"So…did you still do Christmas and stuff or…"

"Yeah, I still got stuff once in a while." I set the wrapped box with her father's slippers to the side. "But it wasn't really fun stuff. It was usually just the essentials that I needed anyway. Socks, my favorite snacks, a new suitcase, stuff like that. When I *would* get a new toy, it would be a single toy while their real kids got several." I shrug again because I feel like I'm bringing down the mood. Dean Martin singing, "A Marshmallow World" doesn't help. "Anyway, I didn't really have traditions, per se, because each year I never knew if I'd be there the following year." Finally, I look up at her and ask, "What do you want me to wrap next?"

There's pity in her eyes and I immediately try to deflect.

"My life wasn't bad. I wasn't ever beaten or any of the horror stories you hear. I had foster parents who cared about me. They were just cautious to get close. I was too. But, I mean, I finished high school okay, I went to college, I have a decent job, a nice place to live, a handful of friends. I'm okay."

Charlotte grabs another gift and hands it to me. "Well good. I'm glad."

Neither of us speak as we go back to wrapping. I feel like I've definitely ruined the mood—and maybe even the status of our relationship. Whatever that may be. I've always been reluctant to get close to people, but Charlotte's different. She never really gave me a choice to get close to her. She has the type of personality that just grabs you and

pulls you in and makes you feel like you've known her for- 95
ever. She makes you want to spend more time with her. To
get to know more about her. It's only fair that I tell her a bit
about myself, too.

"So what made you start writing?" she asks.

Inside, I breathe a sigh of relief that she's changed the
topic. That she's seeing me for who I am and not what I've
been through.

"I've always enjoyed writing. Journaling, telling stories, creating characters in my head. Through the years,
that kind of combined with my curiosity about the world
and I decided to pursue that when I went to college."

She chuckles. "I take it a home design magazine isn't
your dream job."

"Uh, no, not really." I laugh. "I'd love to work for a travel magazine. To be sent on assignments across the world
and *discover* places, you know? Learning about other cul-
tures or rediscovering our own. I think that'd be a really
exciting job. It wouldn't feel like work."

"I could see that." She peels off a tag and reaches down
to stick it on her dad's gift. "You've kind of been a nomad
your whole life."

"I guess you could say that."

"It might also be how you got started with writing," she
adds. "It's a form of escape."

I rub my forehead. I know where she's going with this
now and it's not where I'd hoped it would be. "Could we
not talk about me being in foster care? It's in the past and

I've moved on from it. Really, I'm fine."

"I know you are," she says. "I mean, I've known you a couple months and I had no idea."

I hear the front door open and the Barlows walk in.

"Good thing we're just about done." Maybe ignoring her comments about my past will make her stop. "Sounds like your folks are home."

She looks up to the door. "Guess so."

An instrumental song starts playing, but the silence between us is perhaps the loudest thing in the room.

"I just want you to know that you can talk to me if you want," she says after a while. "I'll listen. God knows I owe it to you after this favor."

"So *that's* why you're going to listen if I want to talk?" I can't ignore the itch anymore. Not when she can't let it go, despite me asking her several times. "Because you *owe* me one?"

"Kaden, that's not what I meant." She looks surprised by my response, which only makes me angrier. "I want to make sure you're okay."

"You just want to help out your little orphan pal who's had such a tough life." I get to my feet.

"That's not at all what I said."

"But that's what you meant. Now that you know about my parents, that's the only way you're going to see me. Broken. I don't need your pity because there's nothing to worry about. I'm *fine*. What this all boils down to is you not wanting to worry about your own damn problems."

I don't wait for her to reply. I storm out of the room, forgetting that we're no longer home alone until I see her parents. Maria's standing in the opening by the kitchen and Jim is looking over his shoulder from the recliner in the living room, the newspaper spread across his lap.

I clear my throat and mutter, "Sorry."

Jim gets up and walks to the door leading to the garage, waving for me to follow. "Come on. I could use your help."

I grab my coat and step into the garage after him. He flicks on the lights and even ignites an electric space heater.

"My own little personal oasis," he says with a grin.

I wait for him to say something about how even he needs an escape once in a while or that everyone needs to be able to let off steam or Christmas is stressful and blah blah blah. But instead he waves me over to several strings of lights lying on the work bench.

"I took these little buggers off last night," he says. "None of them were lighting up. I'm hoping all they need are new fuses. If you help, we should be able to finish before the cold gets to our fingers. What do you say?"

I could use the distraction. "Sure. I've never changed a fuse before. How do you do it?"

"Here, watch."

I step closer so I can see.

"You just pull this tab back like…this, pull out the fuse—" He sets the tiny little fuse down on the work bench and grabs a fresh one. "—put the new one in and slide the tab back. Easy as that." He finds the end and plugs it into an outlet. The whole strand lights up. "Eureka!"

I offer a small smile. Apparently, it's enough.

"So how are things going between you and my daughter?"

I keep my eyes focused on my hands as I work out the next tiny little broken fuse. "They're okay."

"You know, our Char, she hasn't brought a boy home in a while. Not since she moved to the big city."

"Yeah, she told me."

"And Christmas is possibly the worst time to meet someone's family—especially in such a new relationship. It just brings everything to a new level."

What's adding to my stress at the moment is this conversation. But I don't want to be rude, nor do I want to ruin all of this because I'm mad at Charlotte right now, so I keep quiet and let him talk.

"I know I'm kind of a stranger to you, but Charlotte's not," he says. "I care about her and if she cares about you, then so do I. So, if you need to talk or just take five minutes to get away from it all, I'm usually in here or in the recliner with the paper. Even if all you want to do is sit in silence."

I offer him a genuine smile. "Thanks. I appreciate it."

"No pressure. I just thought I'd put it out there." He reaches for another tangled strand. "All right, let's get going on these. I would like to put them back up for the misses in time for Christmas."

❆ ❆ ❆

"YOU ALL SET with the light?" Charlotte asks.

"Yeah, go ahead."

It's the first thing we've said to each other since our little spat earlier. Neither of us said much at dinner. I kept up a brief conversation with Arthur about traffic in a couple different cities: New York, Columbus, Nashville, Boston. All places we've either lived in or visited frequently. That lasted about as long as any conversation about traffic could. Then we were quiet again. Mostly, I just listened in as Olivia tried to get Ken to eat and Maria responded to Maddie's questions about when *exactly* Santa was coming.

After dinner, Jim and I watched TV while Arthur and Olivia put the kids to bed and Charlotte and Maria cleaned up the kitchen, taking a much longer time than they did the last two nights.

Now, the two people who haven't spoken to each other in several hours are less than three feet away from each other, pouting like the couple we supposedly are. What's the rule? Don't go to bed angry? Is that a thing? Does it apply to us?

Almost on cue, Charlotte's quiet voice rises in the darkness.

"I'm sorry for what I said earlier." She pauses, waiting for my response. "Are you still awake?"

"Yeah."

"Oh."

I debate whether I should tell her that it's okay. That what she said was fine because she didn't know. But it bothers me because I don't want her to have a tarnished view of me. Even if we never talk again after this week, I don't want her to think of me as a fragile orphan boy. My past is what I've been through. It's what shaped who I am, but it's not *all* that I am. She needs to know that. Accepting her apology would send a different message.

"I didn't mean to be nosy or to make assumptions about you," she continues. "I'm just trying to figure you out because you *don't* talk about yourself very much. I was surprised by the way you grew up and I was just trying to fill in the pieces."

I close my eyes and consider responding. What she's saying makes sense. I *haven't* talked about myself much, but that's just who I am. I'm not an open book like Charlotte is. Sometimes I wish I could be.

"After you yelled—which I totally understand—I didn't know what to say to make things better," she goes on. "I didn't know if there was anything I *could* say. But I know I needed to say something, so that's what this is. I just wanted you to know where I'm coming from. But I see what you're saying too. I'll try not to look at you any differently than I did before."

Except, I've heard that line before. From other girls. From teachers, friends, even my foster parents. Once they know my story, I'm like a whole new person to them and I hate it. Try as she might, Charlotte is probably not going to see me the same way she did before.

CHRISTMAS EVE
Charlotte

❄ ❄ ❄

Silverware clangs against the plates at breakfast as we each eat in silence. The sun streams through the window onto the table. It's a beautiful day outside, but inside the atmosphere is quite different.

Maddie watches cartoons in the living room while Olivia tries to get both her and the baby to eat some cereal. Dad's reading the newspaper at the end of the table and Arthur scrolls through his phone. I can feel my mother's eyes on me from across the table. Kaden and I focus on our plates, neither one of us daring to look at the other.

I'm more than a little annoyed with him. Sure, I may have crossed a line yesterday, but I apologized for that. Well, tried to. He didn't even have the decency to say *anything* to me after my attempt to smooth things over.

Even this morning, I heard him get up to use the bathroom and I was hoping he'd come back in the room so we could talk a bit more, but he purposely waited for me to come out before he went in to get himself ready for the day. If this is the way he wants to move forward, then fine. Maybe we won't even have a friendship after this week is over.

"I'm heading out to Nancy's house for lunch to open gifts with the girls," Mom says. It's a tradition she has every year with her friends. They have their own Christmas gathering on Christmas Eve morning. "Which means, I'll need everyone's help cleaning up today." Mom rests her chin on her hands over her plate of eggs. "Outside and inside."

"Sounds good," Olivia says.

I nod, but apparently that isn't enough.

"Okay, Charlotte?" She looks annoyed. I wonder if it's because Christmas is tomorrow and nobody's talking. If anything, we look bored.

It's Mom's favorite holiday and while she tries not to have high expectations, she at least wants everyone to have a good time. I guess I can't blame her for that one.

"Yes, Mom." I take a sip of my coffee. It's lukewarm and I only have a little bit left.

"Kaden and Arthur, you boys can help Jim outside."

"Okay." Kaden nods and smiles at her as he chews up the last of his food. It's as if our whole spat yesterday never happened whenever he talks to anyone else. I just want him to talk to me. And to think, I was having such a good day with him before everything went to crap.

"Dinner's at six and I suspect everyone will be over by about five," Mom says. "So Charlotte, I'll need yours and your sister's help cleaning up inside. Maybe even later in the kitchen, too."

"I said okay." It comes off whiny, like I'm a teenager again. Instead of waiting for her retort, I stand, finish off my coffee, and snatch up all the empty plates. "You finished with that?" I ask Kaden directly.

He pushes it in my direction, but keeps his focus on his phone. What a jerk.

I head into the kitchen and get started on the dishes, washing them by hand in order to kill time until Kaden's outside with my dad and Arthur.

"You know we have a dishwasher, dear," Mom says from behind me.

I set the clean dishes in the drying rack and look back at her over my shoulder. "I thought it was clean."

"Then you could've emptied it." She opens it and starts putting away the clean dishes.

"Sorry," I mutter.

"Christmas is tomorrow! Christmas is tomorrow! One more day!" Maddie shrieks as she runs through the house.

Olivia comes in with Ken on her hip. "She's a little excited."

I look back at her and smile. "That's good, though."

"At least *someone* is excited around here," Mom murmurs.

"I'll see if I can con her into doing some chores to help

out," Olivia says. "If not, maybe I can convince her to stick to the living room to keep any new messes to a minimum. That way, maybe I can help, too."

"I've made a list for you girls." Mom pats a scrap piece of paper on the counter. "I don't care who does what, but all of it needs to get done."

I dry my hands and take a look. Nothing too outrageous. Cleaning the kitchen is among them, but with Mom preparing dinner all day, the kitchen is the farthest place I want to be. I know she'll try to figure out what's going on between me and Kaden and I don't want to tell her. Not to mention, cleaning the kitchen is the last thing that needs to be done if Mom's going to be preparing dinner all day. Well, with the exception of the few hours she's gone with her friends.

"I'll get started on the windows." I grab a roll of paper towels and the Windex and start in the living room, watching out the window as Kaden, Arthur, and Dad shovel out the driveway and the front sidewalk. They're each bundled in hats, gloves, scarves, and heavy coats, despite the bright sun.

I love the way my family has so willingly accepted Kaden. I made them believe he was important to me and just like that, he was important to them too. Too bad it's all a lie. Will they act the same with someone I'm actually dating? Will I be okay if they don't? Will I hear about Kaden for the rest of my life as each guy I date is compared to him? Will *I* compare the guys I date in the future to the picture-perfect image Kaden's creating? All of this for my selfish image. I feel like a horrible person.

Once the living room windows are cleaned, I move on through the rest of the house. After that, I pull out the vacuum and make a sweep of the whole house. I find anything I can do to stay out of the kitchen. Baby Ken sleeps in the crib upstairs, but the vacuum doesn't bother him. I pause and watch him sleep for a while.

I would love to be a mother someday. I could picture myself going to soccer practices, parent-teacher conferences, and helping with homework. Even the midnight wake-up calls and endless anxiety about where they are and what they're doing brings a smile to my face. Being a parent sounds like an adventure. One I can tell I'm getting ready for.

Of course, I don't know who I'll be with when I become a mother. I don't know if I'll still be living in New York or even if I'll decide to keep my job. Am I willing to give up something that I've worked so hard for in order to care for something that is still hypothetical?

It's too hard to compare right now. And it's useless to even think about. I'm not really dating anybody, so marriage and kids and my future can wait.

Olivia and I check off everything on Mom's list while she's gone. Just after I make myself a quick sandwich for lunch, the package I ordered yesterday arrives. It's a last-minute present for Kaden. A decision I made while I was wrapped up in guilt for making him mad. For half a second

I consider returning it, but I paid a fortune for rush delivery and there's no way I'd get that money back, so I might as well just give him the gift. I think it'd be perfect anyway.

When Mom comes back home in mid-afternoon, she's pleasantly surprised that all the cleaning's done. Still, she finds things to fuss with in the kitchen, barking orders at me and my sister until it's time for us to get ready.

By nearly five o'clock, the guys have already come back in and gotten ready for the evening's celebrations while us ladies put on our final touches. With the tension between me and Kaden reaching a peak, I head up to my sister's room to borrow some makeup. Arthur's already taken the kids downstairs. Our aunts and uncles should be here anytime now.

"You look nice." Olivia's wearing a green blouse and black pants. Her thick dark hair falls over her shoulders.

"Thanks! So do you." I move to the mirror and start working some extra color onto my cheeks. Not too much, but enough that I don't look like a zombie. I'm in a brown sweater and khakis. Dressy, but still pretty casual.

My sister takes a seat on the bed. It's a small room and between the double bed, the crib, and the dresser, I'm not sure how her, Arthur, and the kids all fit. Especially when it seems that Maddie's been sharing the bed with them.

"Are you okay?" she asks.

"Yeah, I'm fine. Why?"

"Are you and Kaden doing okay? I got the feeling something was up at breakfast and you've kind of been quiet all day."

I close up the products and stow them away. "We just had a little spat. It's not a big deal."

"What was it about?"

I wave it off and take a seat next to her. "It's not a big deal. We'll get over it."

"Oh."

My response apparently doesn't sit well with her. I get it. We used to be really close. I still care a lot about her, but it's different now that we're adults. We're not as involved in our day-to-day lives anymore and it looks like I'm shutting myself off from her by not telling her all about mine and Kaden's fight. Not only is it incredibly personal for Kaden, but I don't want to divulge too much to Olivia because that might raise questions about the authenticity of my relationship. It's better to just play it off as distant.

"You know, I've always looked up to you," Olivia says.

This brings a smile to my face and a giddiness I haven't felt in a long time. "You have?"

"You've always followed your own path," she explains. "You never let anyone tell you what to do. You wanted to be a writer in New York City and you worked at it and that's what you've become."

I roll my eyes and look at my hands. "Tell that to Mom."

"You mean the dating thing?"

"Yeah."

"She'll get over it. Besides, I've always admired that part of you too. You didn't need to find a partner for your own validation. I know I was giving you a little bit of a hard time about being single, but I love it that you created the life you wanted for yourself before you found a partner. And he's a good one, too."

My smile softens. I wonder what she'd think of me if she knew that mine and Kaden's relationship was fake. She just told me that she likes that I've never done anything to please other people and yet I'm masquerading as a woman in a relationship in order to appease my family. I'm a fraud.

"That still doesn't stop Mom from saying—"

"Forget what Mom says," Olivia cuts me off. "What do *you* want? Do you even want a husband and kids?"

I consider that. "Yeah, I do. But starting a family has always been on the backburner, you know? I always tell myself, *You have time for all of that.* But what if the opportunity passes me by completely?"

She scooches closer to me and leans her head on my shoulder. "I've never once regretted my relationship with my husband or the kids we've had, but sometimes I do wish I had taken more time for myself first. That's why I'm glad you didn't listen to Mom or anyone else until you found someone who could fit into the lifestyle *you* created for yourself."

My eyes well up and I look away. My sister doesn't know me at all like I thought she did and it's my fault.

How could I do this to my family? I'm purposely putting distance between us.

She wraps her arms around me and squeezes. "Aw, don't cry. It's okay. I was really happy to see Kaden here. It just means that you haven't given up on finding someone and maybe starting a family, even though you're focused on your job."

I dab at my eyes so my tears don't ruin my newly-applied makeup, but they still come. Olivia's right. I haven't given up on that dream, but as time goes on, it seems less likely of becoming a reality. As of right now, Kaden's the closest thing I have to a boyfriend and that's not even real. It doesn't help that he's not talking to me.

Will my family start to look at me with pity if I never marry or have kids? I don't want them to see me any differently. I'm still me.

Just like Kaden said yesterday. Now I know what it feels like. It sucks.

"Even if settling down isn't on your mind right now, you should just ride the wave with Kaden and see where it takes you," Olivia says. "If it doesn't work out, it doesn't work out. But give it your best shot while he's here."

I exhale heavily. "Thanks. You're right. I should try to figure out where things stand with us."

At the very least, I should apologize again and let him know that I got a glimpse of what he's been feeling all his life. And to be honest, I really lucked out with my fake boyfriend. Olivia's right: he's a good one. Too bad I probably messed up whatever chances I might've had with him for real. If I were him, I'd be running away from me so fast after this week.

Our mother shrieks with joy from downstairs and the volume from the first floor jumps up as our two aunts and their husbands arrive.

"Guess we better get down there," Olivia says.

I dab at my eyes. "Guess so. Thanks."

"Of course. Anytime you want to talk, just give me a call."

Almost on cue, Ken starts crying downstairs.

"If you can handle the occasional freak out over the phone," she adds.

I laugh. "I think I can deal with that."

Downstairs, Dad, Arthur, Uncle Geoff, and Uncle Pete have all plopped themselves in the living room. In the kitchen, Mom works on dinner while Aunt Rose and Aunt Linda interrogate Kaden in the dining room. I consider letting them at him, but decide that's too cruel. He's already suffered through at least five minutes of questions. I promised him I'd try to keep them away from him.

I give both of my aunts hugs and then sit beside Kaden at the table, letting my hand trail across his shoulder as I take a seat. Hopefully, that'll be a clue for him that I'm not mad at him. He looks surprised, but grateful to see me.

"You never said you had a *boyfriend*," Aunt Rose says with a smirk.

"*Very* cute, but very quiet—good catch, dear," Aunt

Linda adds. She nudges her sister and they both erupt in cackles. "Good listeners are the best. You know, it's the quiet ones you have watch out for. They're always the most…surprising."

More laughs as Kaden's face turns a shade darker.

"I heard you've only recently gotten together," Aunt Rose says. "Bringing him home for the family Christmas? That's a very big step."

"I didn't meet Petey's family until after I was pregnant," Aunt Linda says.

"So that would've been—what?—your second date?" Aunt Rose asks.

Aunt Linda gasps and smacks her sister's arm. "You're *bad*. It was our third."

Olivia and I join in with the laughter. My aunts have so much energy, especially when they get together. I'm usually sore the next day from laughing so much.

"What are you two hens chatting about?" Dad steps in from the living room. He tips his head back to finish what's left of his beer. He pats my shoulder. "You girls look nice."

"Thanks, Dad." Olivia and I both say.

"We're just getting to know our niece's new man," Aunt Linda tells him. "You should be glad she brought home a good one."

He shrugs. "I'm just happy I don't need to hear Maria complain that the family pictures are uneven anymore."

"I heard that!" Mom calls from the kitchen.

Dad disappears to grab another bottle of beer from the fridge.

"Have they driven you crazy yet?" Aunt Rose asks Kaden in a mock-whisper.

He smiles politely. "Everyone's been really nice."

She waves her hand at him. "Eh, you haven't seen who they *really* are then."

"Well, do you think he's even seen the real Char yet?" Aunt Linda asks her.

Dad comes back in and takes a seat at the table.

"No," Aunt Rose responds. "The girl has common sense. She's not going to pull the crazy card until there's a big fat ring on her finger." She turns and shouts over her shoulder, "Isn't that right, dear?"

"Yes, honey," Uncle Geoff drones.

Everyone laughs.

"I could use some help in here," Maria says.

"Kaden," Olivia says quickly. "Why don't you and I help?"

He quickly pops up from his seat and follows my sister into the kitchen.

"Don't worry, we're not going anywhere," Aunt Rose calls after him.

Aunt Linda turns to me. "Are you happy, dear?"

A loaded question that requires another lie, but they didn't ask about Kaden specifically so I guess it's technically the truth.

"Yes," I say with a convincing smile.

"Good," she says. "He seems like a very nice young man."

"He is," I say.

"I'm just not sure he'll be able to keep up with this family," Aunt Rose says. "You'll have to whip him into shape like the rest of us did with our men. Isn't that right, Jim?"

"It'd help if he develops a mild hearing problem," Dad says, which receives a playful smack from Aunt Rose.

"Charlotte, dear, can you set the table?" Mom calls over the stove fan.

I head into the hot kitchen. Mom has the oven open and the smell of turkey grows stronger. I grab a stack of plates and silverware from the cupboard and follow Kaden, who's carrying the stuffing, out to the dining room.

"Ah!" Aunt Rose calls. "Look what you two walked under!"

I didn't even notice the mistletoe earlier. Mom never usually hangs it.

"It was my little gift," Aunt Linda explains. "Looks like it came in handy, too."

I set the dishes down on the table and try to ignore it. "It looks nice."

Kaden's red in the face, but I don't draw attention to it.

"Come on," Aunt Rose pushes. "Just one little peck. Enjoy it while you've still got the heat."

Now I'm sure my face is just as red as Kaden's, especially with everyone's eyes on us. We had agreed that there'd be no kissing. That was where we drew the line. But Kaden's walking up to me, stepping closer until he's all I can see. My heart races as I look into his eyes.

I lean to my right, he leans to his left and we bang out foreheads against each other. Not the cinematic moment I pictured in my head.

My aunts laugh.

We quickly readjust and complete the quickest kiss in history, pulling away almost instantly. That's a moment I'm never going to live down.

I return to the kitchen, burning with embarrassment as my aunts cheer behind me. My heart pounds in my chest and I feel an overwhelming sense of fear because of how much I liked kissing Kaden.

CHRISTMAS DAY
Kaden

I stretch out on the floor in the morning under the blankets but quickly draw my limbs back in, shivering. It was exceptionally cold last night and the constant blast from the heating vent wasn't enough to take the chill out.

Pulling the blankets up to my chin, I stare up at the ceiling and try to beat away the thoughts floating in my head. The ones that have been present since the kiss Charlotte and I shared last night.

It was awkward and clumsy and certainly looked more like the nervous first kiss that it was rather than just another kiss between two people in a budding romance, which it was supposed to be. Nobody said anything about it, though. But then, dinner was served shortly after and the topic of conversation quickly changed to Baby Ken.

Thank God.

Charlotte and I didn't say much to each other the rest of the night, although I can honestly say that any animosity I had toward her is gone after that kiss, replaced instead by the growing lust that started back in New York. I know it will fade when we return home, though, but for the moment, she's all I can think about.

I'm pulled out of my head when I hear quick footsteps cascading down the stairs. I don't know whether it's wishful thinking or impulse, but I jump to my feet, grabbing the extra blankets, and hop over Charlotte's sleeping form on the bed and press my body against hers in an effort to look natural.

She stirs, but before she says anything, Maddie bounds in the room.

"It's CHRISTMAS!"

Charlotte sits up and thoroughly looks confused. I smile down at her niece and say, "Merry Christmas, Maddie!"

"Get up! Get up! Get up!" she demands. "Come on! It's time to open presents!"

"Okay," Charlotte says hoarsely. "Give us a few minutes and we'll be out there."

The girl turns and races out the door, running to Mr. and Mrs. Barlow's bedroom next.

Charlotte looks back at me but doesn't say anything. She just waves her hand between us and gives a worried look.

"I heard her coming and thought we better make it look like we're sharing a bed," I say. The last thing I want is for Charlotte to think that I'm taking advantage of her. Especially if she thinks the kiss is the reason. I liked it, but I wouldn't cross that line without her permission.

"Oh." She nods slowly, still confused. "Okay."

"Yeah." I slide to the end of the bed and get to my feet. "Sorry for waking you."

"No, it's okay." She pushes her messy hair out of her face. "It was probably a smart move anyway. Maddie wouldn't let it go if she had a question about something."

"All right, all right, we're coming!" Mr. Barlow's voice carries down the hallway.

I nod to the living room. "We should get going before we have an angry four-year-old on our hands."

"You're right."

I pad out to the living room where the rest of Charlotte's family has already gathered, groggy but smiling at Maddie's excitement.

"Merry Christmas, young man." Mr. Barlow gives me a firm handshake. He's in a gray bathrobe and brown worn-out slippers.

Olivia smiles at me when I step into the kitchen for some coffee. "Good morning and Merry Christmas!"

"Merry Christmas," I reply.

Charlotte's mom gives me a quick hug. "It's Christmas, so you're family for today. I don't care what my daughter says otherwise."

That brings a smile to my face. "Thanks. I appreciate that." I move to the counter and fill two mugs with coffee. I add the extras into Charlotte's just how she likes it.

Maria waves us to the living room. "Come on, Maddie's anxious to open her presents."

"Mom, she can wait until we all open ours," Olivia says.

"Nonsense." Maria takes a seat on the couch, careful not to spill her coffee. "It's Christmas. Let the girl indulge a little. We can wait until after breakfast for the rest of us, if you'd like."

"Plus, it'll keep her quiet while we eat," Mr. Barlow adds.

"She's not a *dog*, Jim," Maria retorts.

Charlotte comes out of the bedroom in a white bathrobe. She rubs her forehead and shuffles her feet. I wonder if she's not feeling well. Regret?

"Come sit, dear," her mother calls to her. "Maddie's patiently waiting."

The blonde four-year-old is kneeling on the floor with her baby brother propped up against her legs. In front of her, Olivia holds up her phone to take pictures. Arthur stands behind his wife, snapping and making faces to try to get Ken's attention for the camera.

"Let me just grab some coffee," Charlotte says.

I hold up the second mug. "Already got you some."

"Did you add anything?"

I nod. "Yup. Your usual."

"Sugar?"

"Two scoops."

"Cream?"

"Just a little."

"Wow. You remembered." She comes over and squeezes on the couch between me and her mother.

"Oh, take advantage of *that* while you still can," Olivia mutters.

"What's that supposed to mean?" Arthur asks with a smirk.

She leans back, apparently satisfied with her pictures. "Nothing, honey."

"Can I start?" Maddie asks excitedly after her dad has pulled Baby Ken away from her lap.

Olivia smiles and looks around the room. "I don't know, is everyone ready?"

Maria rolls her eyes. "Oh, stop teasing her!"

"Okay, grab one and tell us who it's from," Olivia says.

Maddie goes straight for the biggest box wrapped in red paper. "This one's from Grandma and Grandpa!" She looks at her mom, who counts down from three and starts tearing into the paper as soon as she hears, "Go!"

Maddie's squeals could break glass, but it's her uncontrollable excitement that brings a smile to everyone's faces. She shakes and jumps with the present half-open as she screams, "IT'S A DOLLHOUSE!"

"Why don't you say thank you to Grandma and Grandpa," Olivia urges.

Maddie runs over and hugs both grandparents before

bolting back and tearing through the rest of the paper, revealing the magnificent dollhouse that stands up to her shoulder.

Even though I've had so many temporary families in my life, this one feels different. I'm not singled out by getting more or less attention than everyone else. Under the disguise of Charlotte's partner, I'm no different than Arthur is right now or even Jim was last night with Maria's sisters. This is a new way to celebrate the holiday, and even though it's only eight o'clock in the morning, it's already the best Christmas I can remember having in a long time.

After Maddie has torn through all of her presents, the girls head into the kitchen to make breakfast while Jim, Arthur, and I sit in the living room and watch the kids.

Baby Ken lays on Jim's lap and within a few minutes, both of them are asleep.

"Bet this wasn't how you were expecting to spend Christmas this year, huh?" Arthur asks.

I shrug. "It's not bad, actually."

"She gets a little too excited sometimes," he says with a chuckle. "Isn't that right, Mads?"

She's crouched on the floor playing with her new dollhouse. It worked out well that it was the first gift she opened because a lot of the following gifts were things to put inside her toy house.

She sighs heavily.

Arthur looks up. "What's the matter, sweetheart?"

"Nothing."

"Don't you like your dollhouse?"

"I do, but I wish I had someone to play with." She looks up at me. "Mr. Kaden, do you want to play?"

I stare at her with my mouth open. I've never really played with a little girl before. Well, not since I was a little boy.

"You don't have to," Arthur murmurs.

I see the smile start to fade from Maddie's face and I get down on the floor next to her.

"What are we playing?"

She hands me a male doll. "Here, you can be the daddy."

"Who are you going to be, then?" I try to remember the way Charlotte was playing with her the other day. Just ask questions and let Maddie make up her own stories. Plus, playing with dolls is essentially just playing house. Easy enough.

"I'll be the mommy. You need to go shovel the snow. I'm going in the hot tub."

I move the doll around to make it look like he's shoveling. After a few seconds I say, "All done."

She puts a finger on her chin. "Hmm…looks like there's still some snow left. You better go back out and keep shoveling. And don't track the snow in the house!"

Arthur chuckles behind me, but I ignore him. It's a little embarrassing to be playing with dolls, but Maddie's making me laugh, so I don't mind too much.

Eventually, Olivia calls from the kitchen that breakfast is ready.

"This looks delicious," I say as I take my seat next to Charlotte.

"Thank you," Maria says. "It's nothing special. Just some eggs, toast, and sausage."

"You're spoiling me with all these home-cooked breakfasts. Before this week, I hadn't had something hot for breakfast in years." I reach for the butter to spread on my toast.

"Oh, I'm glad you like it, dear," Maria says.

"Is that some New Yorker thing?" Seated at the head of the table, Jim reaches in front of him to scoop some of the scrambled eggs onto his plate.

"It's an I'm-too-lazy-to-cook-for-myself-in-the-morning thing."

Everyone laughs and we all fill our plates.

"Are you okay, Char?" Olivia asks. She steals a look up at her sister while trying to get Baby Ken to eat some eggs.

"Yeah, why?"

"You seem off today, dear," Maria adds. "Are you sick?"

She shakes her head and forces a smile. "No. I just had a weird dream last night, that's all. It's been on my mind since I woke up."

"Was it a *good* dream?" Olivia asks with a giggle.

"Oh, honey!" Maria cries.

Jim laughs. "Must be she woke up here and it made her depressed."

Maria looks at Charlotte. "Don't listen to them, dear. Just have some more to eat and you'll be all better." She turns to her granddaughter. "Do you like all your new toys, sweetheart?"

Maddie nods. "Mm-hmm. Mr. Kaden was playing with me."

I can feel Charlotte's eyes on me, but it's Olivia who speaks up.

"Oh he was, was he?"

"Yeah, he was the daddy and he needed to shovel snow. I went in the hot tub because it's cold outside."

Olivia smiles. "Well, I'm glad you had fun. Maybe he can play with you some more later."

After breakfast, we all break up back into our rooms to change out of our pajamas. Charlotte and I take turns pulling our clothes for the day out of the one dresser in the small bedroom. As I'm pulling my clothes out, she clears her throat.

"You know, um, if you want, you don't have to sleep on the floor tonight." Her eyes survey the bed, the blankets still tangled together from this morning. "I didn't realize how much room there really was until you—until this morning. So, maybe for the rest of the week I could, uh, share. If that's okay," she adds quickly. "No pressure, I just thought—I mean, the floor seemed pretty chilly this morning when I woke up and I can't imagine that's very *healthy*, but..." Her voice trails off.

I look at her in silence. I don't know what to say. I'm surprised she's offering and I'm excited by the idea, but I don't know if I should take her up on it. We never really established what our intentions were for after this week and I don't want to complicate things with a coworker more than I already have. We've already crossed the one line we drew.

What's next? What happens if all of these feelings disappear once we return to our routines? What if they don't disappear for one of us?

"Um, yeah," I finally say. "I'll see where we're at tonight." That'll give me some time to roll it over in my head before I jump into bed with her. Literally.

Her smile fades. "Yeah, that's fine. Do you want to change in here or the bathroom?"

Dammit. Did I just mess things up? Did she *want* me to sleep with her? In the bed, that is. What other rules went out the window with that kiss?

"Kaden?"

I snap out of it. "Oh. Sorry. Doesn't matter to me. You can stay here. I'll take the bathroom." I snatch up my clothes and head to the door, but stop before I leave. I need to give her something. Something so she's not disappointed on Christmas. Or ever. "That kiss last night was—"

"Kinda weird, right?" She oversells a laugh.

I smirk. "Yeah, but it was also really nice. Too bad there were so many people around."

She stares at me and I give her a smile before leaving the room.

❄ ❄ ❄

WE'RE ALL CROWDED in the living room again as we pass out presents. It's not as organized as it was when Maddie was the only one opening hers. Despite the lack of shrieks and howls and jumping, the room is chaotic with gifts being traded, layers of paper covering the floor, and piles of gifts being stashed wherever there's room until the next gift arrives.

To my complete surprise, I get a gift from everyone. Olivia and Arthur got me "gourmet" coffee with a large fancy mug. I unwrapped a nice leather-bound notebook and a ballpoint pen from Maria and Jim. What else do you get the writer you don't really know that well?

To my biggest surprise, Charlotte sets a large gift bag in front of me. "To you from me."

If it's possible, somehow I smile even wider. "When did you get this?" We've been together basically twenty-four seven since Saturday.

"When the line was *so long* at the mall," she admits.

I let my smile slip away for a second. "So you lied to me?"

She rolls her eyes. "Just open it."

I push aside the tissue paper and pull each gift out: a blue paisley tie, striped dress socks, and a black bag.

"The tie is because I think you look good in blue," she says. "And everyone needs socks."

"And this?" I hold up the bag.

"It's for your camera—when you get one—for when you get that dream travel job you want," she explains. "I thought it might be a helpful motivation…and I couldn't exactly afford the camera just yet."

"Thank you. I love it." I reach over and give her a big hug, kissing her on the cheek before we part. She doesn't react to the kiss. Is she acting or genuinely that comfortable with me now?

"What happened to your gift wrapping standards?" I ask, holding up the empty gift bag.

Her face goes red. "I did overnight delivery for this one," she explains. "I was just so happy it came in time and I was in a rush."

"At least I took the time to wrap mine." I pull a small box covered in blue wrapping paper with snowflakes out of the edge of the cushion and hand it to her. "It's not really as thoughtful as your gift, but I hope you like it."

She tears into the paper and her eyes flash up at me with a mix of panic and excitement when she reveals a large jewelry box.

"Open it."

When she does, she gasps.

"What is it?" Olivia asks. I hadn't realized everyone was watching us.

Immediately, Charlotte pulls out the gold necklace I got her with a matching locket on the end.

"Oooo, that's pretty," Maria says.

"I didn't know what picture you'd want inside, so it's blank," I say. "I hope you like it, though."

She pulls me in for another hug, tighter than the one

we just shared. She mutters in my ear, "You're just full of surprises, aren't you?"

When we pull away, she looks at me, then grabs my chin with her hand and kisses me right on the lips. I'm not sure for how long, since the blood seems to rush out of my head, but it's enough to get everyone's attention.

"Don't give away the farm, dear, it's just a necklace," Maria mutters.

Charlotte pulls away and we chuckle between us. There's something here. Something that wasn't here last week, back when she was almost a total stranger. How did my world change so much so fast? Thank God it did, though.

After we clean up the living room, we settle in on the couch—Charlotte even pulls my arm around her so she's laying on top of me—and watch Maddie play with her toys some more.

"Mr. Kaden, do you want to play with me again?" Maddie asks.

Olivia glances at me and Charlotte tangled together on the couch. "Why don't you ask Daddy to play with you?" She smacks her husband's knee and he takes the hint and slides on the floor by his daughter.

"Why don't I be the daddy this time? I have such good experience."

Maddie considers this. "No, you can be Miss Cooper." She hands him a doll.

Maria laughs. "Guess you need a bit more experience."

"No more kids," Olivia says.

"Oh, so we'll be waiting a while for a new addition." Maria looks over at Charlotte. "How's Candace doing? Did you see the baby?"

She shakes her head in the crook of my arm. "No, they left him with Jamie's mom."

"Her husband?"

"Yeah."

"Aw, well that's a shame."

"I know," Charlotte admits. "I was hoping to see him. I've only seen pictures. They probably didn't even realize it."

"It's just a sign that you should come home more often," Maria adds.

"Maybe she'll have more surprises," Jim mutters.

"What?" Maria asks.

He shrugs it off.

"Anyway, are you going to have room for all of this stuff on the way home?" Charlotte asks her sister.

"Yeah, we'll be fine."

"Oh! Right!"

"It got here somehow," I add.

"Santa brought it!" Maddie corrects.

My face goes red, afraid I almost blew the secret. "You're right. It was Santa."

"He brought just enough to make sure we could get it all home." Arthur smooths out his daughter's hair.

By late-afternoon, Maria gets up to put the casserole in

the oven for dinner.

"Ugh, more food," Olivia groans. "I'm still stuffed from last night."

"Isn't that what Christmas is about?" Charlotte laughs.

"Yeah, because I'm sure everyone pigged out in the manger during the first Christmas," I add.

The girls laugh.

"It should only be about twenty minutes," Maria announces when she returns. "Everything's already cooked. It just needs to be heated up." She swats her husband's leg. "What's the matter, honey? You're kind of quiet today."

"Sorry." He nods to us. "So, uh, you two seem to be getting along better."

Charlotte hangs on my arm. "It's a special day."

"True. How long have you been dating?"

She pauses and her brow crinkles. "A month."

He points up at me. "I was asking him."

Everyone turns to look at Mr. Barlow.

Maria swats his leg again. "They already told us that, Jim."

"I know, I know, I'm just asking," he says. "They just seem to suddenly be all over each other when all this week they seemed like strangers."

Charlotte untangles herself from me.

"Jim, what are you doing?" Maria asks. The room seems quiet and stiff now.

"I'm just not sure everyone's being honest here, that's all," he says.

I study the floor. There's a piece of tape stuck to the carpet that we missed when we were cleaning up. It's right there by my foot, but I don't move to grab it.

"What are you talking about?" Maria asks. "Who's not being honest?"

"Nothing." He stands up and points to me and Charlotte. "I need to talk to you two in private." He stalks off out of the room. Seconds later, we hear the door to the garage slam shut.

Charlotte and I exchange glances and ignore the rest of the looks in the room.

"What's going on, guys?" Olivia asks.

Neither of us respond. We're too worried about what her father will say. Earlier, I thought we were on the path to something really special. Now, I'm worried that whatever fragile connection we have will forever be shattered.

Reluctantly, I get up and follow Charlotte out to the garage.

CHRISTMAS DAY
Charlotte

❆ ❆ ❆

The door to the house slams shut behind us as we step into the cold garage. Dad's got his space heater on in the corner on the workbench, but it's not enough to keep the chill out of the whole room. I should've grabbed my coat, but I was hoping we wouldn't be out here long. Dad's expression says otherwise, though.

I steal a glance at Kaden. He looks nervous, but his eyes are on me. Maybe he's more worried about what I'm feeling. After all, he gets to walk away from all of this. I'm the one who has to face this over and over again.

Dad leans against the workbench with one hand and the other rests on his hip. He stares at the concrete floor and doesn't say a word. He's angry and I'm afraid I know exactly what it's about.

"You want to tell me what's going on?" he finally asks. There's still an edge behind his words but his voice is quiet. "I want the truth this time."

Kaden and I look at each other again. I should be the one to say something because this is my family, but I can't. I'm frozen, which has nothing to do with the cold. I don't know what to say because at this point, none of this makes sense anymore. How could I think that I would get away with this?

Dad pounds the work bench. "*Something's* going on!"

His outburst makes me jump.

He turns to me. "You've never lied to me before, Charlotte. I know for a fact that you are now."

That's a punch in the gut I wasn't expecting. I *haven't* lied to my parents before. Never. And yet, lying to them this week came off so easily. Who have I become?

"Kaden and I aren't together," I say in a shaky voice. "I asked him to pretend we were so that—" So that my mother could get off my back? That's not going to be a good enough excuse for Dad.

"So that *what*?" he pushes.

I swallow hard. My hands feel like icicles. "Lately, I've felt like there's a disconnect between me and the rest of the family. And, well, Mom's been saying that I should get a boyfriend and I just thought—"

"Don't put this on your mother," he says. "She didn't ask you to lie to us." He shakes his head and turns away, diverting his eyes from me. "I'm really disappointed in you, Charlotte."

My voice cracks. "I'm sorry, Dad. I know I shouldn't

have done it. I just thought that for one week it wouldn't be so bad. I thought if I told you guys later over the phone that Kaden and I broke up, that this would all just go away. I didn't mean to hurt anyone."

"But you *lied* to us," he says.

I sniffle. "I'm sorry. I know I shouldn't have, but please don't tell anyone else. I don't want to ruin their Christmas. I just want to go back to New York and—"

"And what? Ignore us again?" he asks. "Charlotte, if there's a disconnect between us, it's because ever since you moved away, we only get the occasional phone call and brief updates about how you're doing. Why do you think your mother is so insistent on seeing you with somebody? She thinks that once you find someone to settle down with, you'll move back home and maybe we'll see you more than a couple times a year."

His words hit me like a smack in the face. He's not wrong. I haven't been involved with the family as much as I used to be, but I always thought that was just what happened when you grew up. But then, Olivia does seem to talk to Mom and Dad a lot. I always thought that's because she has kids, but maybe it's just because she's a better person than I am. My sister would never lie to our parents like I did.

"Can I say something?" Kaden asks. He doesn't wait for permission before he continues. "I haven't known Charlotte—or this family—for long, but I did get a glimpse of who she was back in New York. She's well-respected at her job, where she has good friends and she's happy. What she wasn't happy with was that she felt like she couldn't share any of that with her family. So she came up with this plan—albeit kind of haphazardly—in order to appease you guys for a little bit. It wasn't smart, but it's what she felt she had to do because the real Charlotte doesn't feel like she's been getting enough of your attention on her own."

Dad studies him when he's done. What Kaden said was really sweet—and really on point—but I don't know if it's enough for Dad to get over the fact that I've been lying to everyone. I've betrayed his trust.

The door to the house swings open and Mom asks, "What's going on?" She folds her arms to keep warm.

Olivia follows her out and pulls the sleeves of her sweater over her hands.

I look to Dad to see if he'll keep the secret or tell them, even though I know exactly what he's going to do.

He sighs heavily as he looks at me, then turns to Mom and says, "These two are not together."

Mom's brow furrows and she looks between me and Kaden. "Did you break up?"

Olivia steps closer to me, but I shake my head slightly and she stops.

"What's going on?" she asks.

"Go on, tell them," Dad says to me.

"We weren't ever dating," I choke out. "I just said we were because..." I shrug.

Mom continues to look between me, Dad, and Kaden.

"Why would you say you were together if you weren't?" she asks. "And who is this, then?"

"He's…a friend." I'd say that's a safe assumption at this point. "I convinced him to come home with me and pretend to be my boyfriend."

"But *why*, Charlotte?" Olivia crosses her arms to keep warm.

I breathe in a deep breath. "I'm just tired of being judged based off of my relationship status. I'm not getting married or having kids as quickly as you did because we're two different people. Right now, my job is my focus and I've been doing really well there. But every time I talk to Mom it's always about whether or not I'm with someone." I turn to my mother. "You don't even *ask* about work."

The pity I just had for myself turns into a flash of anger. I look over at my dad.

"And you're no help, either. You want to see me more than a few times a year? Take me up on the countless offers I've given you to come visit me in New York. You both seem revolted by the idea of the city, but that's where I live. You make an effort to go see Olivia all the time, I think you can do the same for me."

The garage goes silent as we all take in what I just said. It was bold, that's for sure. I don't want it to sound like I'm trying to turn things around on them, but I want them to know where I'm coming from. Relationships—whether they're romantic or not—are two-way streets.

"We've asked you about your job," Mom says quietly.

"You ask me how work is going, but then quickly change the subject," I say. "I get it, you don't know much about what I do, but asking me questions about it is a good way to learn."

"That has nothing to do with you lying to us all week," Dad says. "You should—"

"Jim." Mom puts up her hand to stop him and steps over to me. "I'm sorry for making you feel like the only way you could fit in with us is to lie about who you are. I've just always wanted you to be happy."

"I am happy, Mom. And I know you want to see the mother in me come out someday, but it's not time yet. And I'm sorry for lying to you." I look around. "All of you."

Mom gives me a hug. "Looks like we'll have to make some changes. I don't ever want you to feel like you need to put on a show for us."

"Thanks." I look over at Dad and say, "Do you mind if we head back inside? It's freezing out here."

He studies me for a moment and then nods. "Go on. I'll be in in a minute."

"Dinner is all set, dear," Mom tells me as I head inside.

"Okay." I motion toward my room. "Just give me a minute, okay?"

"Oh, sure," she says. "Take your time."

"Hey." Olivia gives me a hug once we're back inside. "You okay?"

I nod. "Yeah. Just embarrassing, you know?"

"For what it's worth, I think Mom and Dad got the

message." She turns to Kaden and says, "Kudos to you for putting up with all of this even though you guys aren't actually together."

I turn away.

"Sorry," Olivia says.

"It's okay."

It's good to have Olivia back. When she's not just my sister, but my friend too. The few serious conversations we've had in the last twenty-four hours were exactly what we needed to restore the close bond we had before. Things aren't completely back to the way they used to be, but we're heading in the right direction.

"Can we have a minute?" Kaden asks her.

"Sure." She steps into the kitchen.

"You want to talk?" he asks once she's gone.

I turn to our room. "Not now, Kaden. I'm sorry." I feel horrible for dragging him into this. And I don't even know where to begin to apologize to him.

He nods. "Oh. Okay. Well, I'm here whenever you're ready to talk."

"Thanks."

I leave the door open to our room and lay on the bed on my stomach. I pull out my phone and scroll through the apps. I need a distraction, but my mind's still wrapped up in what just happened. I feel a mixture of relief and embarrassment. Olivia's right. The message got through and I'm sure things are going to change but they're not going to happen overnight. And Kaden's still here and I don't know if I should buy him a ticket home or let him stay the rest of the week. I don't really know who he is to me. Where does he fit in now that he's no longer my boyfriend?

Or, my fake-boyfriend, rather. He wasn't ever *actually* my boyfriend, as much as I might've thought he could be today. I called him a friend earlier, but is that even right? Friends don't kiss each other like we've been.

"Hey," Arthur says from the doorway. "I'm supposed to tell you that dinner's ready."

I readjust so I'm sitting on the edge of the bed. "Yeah, I'll be there in a second."

"Are you okay? Olivia told me real quick what happened."

I shrug. "And now everyone knows how desperate I am."

He comes in and takes a seat next to me. "I wouldn't say you were desperate."

"What else would you call a woman who bribes a man to be her boyfriend? If that doesn't scream future crazy cat lady, I don't know what does."

He chuckles. "I know you and I haven't really talked that much, but I've always kind of admired you."

"Okay," I say sarcastically. He's just trying to cheer me up.

"I'm not kidding. Back when Olivia and I first started dating, she used to tell me about all of your passions and dreams—and then you went and pursued them. I always thought that was very cool."

I smile. "Thanks."

"And I'm really glad that Maddie can grow up with role models for different kinds of women. Olivia will probably go back to work, but being a homemaker is what she's most passionate about. You, on the other hand, even if you do become a mother when you're ready, I know you'll still stay focused on your dreams and I'm really glad that Maddie will get to see that."

"You think I'm going to have that much of an impact on her?"

"Absolutely," he says. "Olivia talks about you all the time. When Maddie gets a little older, she'll know how awesome her aunt is, even if she doesn't see her every day."

I don't know what to say, so I just smile.

Someone knocks on the door and Kaden pokes his head through. "Can I come in?"

Christmas Day
Kaden

❄ ❄ ❄

Arthur gets to his feet and passes by me on his way out the door. "Sure, yeah. Dinner's ready, whenever you want to come out."

"Thanks again," Charlotte tells him. He gives her a wave and leaves us alone.

I take a seat next to her. "Hey."

"Hey," she repeats.

"So the secret's out."

"Guess so."

"How are you doing?"

She shrugs. "Embarrassed, mostly."

"It sounds like your mom's going to make an effort, at least. That's gotta count for something."

"Yeah, it does. I just feel bad for you." She looks over at me. "I'm sorry for ruining your Christmas. Even though you said you didn't have much else planned, you probably could've done without the family drama."

I shake my head and take her hand, but she pulls it away.

"You don't have to do that anymore," she says. "The secret's out, remember?"

I reach for her hand again. "I know. I want to."

She studies me.

"And don't feel bad about getting me involved in this," I say. "All thing's considered, it's been fun."

She hooks an eyebrow. "Really?"

I chuckle. "Well, there were some tense moments, I'll give you that, but it's *mostly* been fun."

She smiles. I wonder if she realizes what I'm getting at. Probably.

"Oh yeah?" she asks. "Like what?"

I squeeze her hand tighter. "Like this. And this morning. I know we were supposed to be pretending but I wasn't. Not really."

Her smile fades as she studies our hands. "What are you saying?"

For a second I wonder if she wasn't actually feeling the same things as me. Maybe she's just a really good actor. But I've already started to tell her how I feel. I can't take back what's already been said.

"You remember last week when I asked you out? You

thought it was a date, but I told you it was for the blog posts." I shake my head. "You were right. I meant it as a date. It's just that when you turned me down, I kind of had no choice but to come up with another excuse."

She smiles but keeps her eyes down. "Oh."

"Yeah. And at the risk of sounding creepy, I've been admiring you for weeks. I've just been trying to build up the courage to ask you out." I shrug. "Susan's assignment was the perfect excuse to talk to you."

"Well, I had no idea—other than when I thought you were asking me out. I just thought that was a way to butter me up in time for New Year's. I figured by time January second came around I'd never hear from you again or something."

I scoff. "Oh gee, thanks. I'm glad you had such a high opinion of me."

She breathes in a deep breath. "To be honest, I had subconsciously sworn off guys because I thought that if I stayed single, I'd stay focused on my ultimate goal. I keep thinking that each new promotion I get will *finally* make me happy. Well, happier than I've been."

"You're not happy?"

"I am, but it just seems like something's not quite clicking into place, you know? Like there's something missing or something in my life needs to be modified."

I smile. "You're talking about me."

She rolls her eyes. "Not you specifically. Well, maybe you. I don't know."

"What do you mean *maybe*?"

Charlotte shrugs. "We've learned a lot about each other this past week. You've been a true gentleman and so good with my family and making sure that I'm having a good time. I guess I've sort of developed a crush on you."

I try to contain my smile now, but I fail miserably. "Since I asked you out, you kind of already know where I stand."

"Yeah."

"Kissing you was nice."

She nods. "Yeah, it was."

"So…where does that leave us?"

"I don't know," she says with a heavy breath. "I don't know if what I'm feeling are genuine feelings or if it's just a byproduct of the week, you know? It's not really natural for two people to be shoved so close together so fast and get to know each other so quickly."

"But," I offer as a rebuttal, "we *did* learn a lot about each other and that wouldn't have happened if we didn't actually care about each other."

And despite the many people who've been in my life, I've never felt a connection like this with anyone other than Charlotte. Okay, so she made some assumptions she shouldn't have when I first told her about my past, but we've already dealt with that. In the last few days, it's obvious that she still cares for me. The fact that she knows my story and is still interested in dating *me* and the person I am makes me want to explore where else this could go.

Charlotte looks in my eyes. "I guess you're right. And you've been really sweet this whole week, going along with this even though you weren't so sure at first. I really appreciate that."

She leans into me and our lips meet. It's the first kiss we've shared that doesn't have an audience. It's the first one that could potentially last a little longer. But then, with Charlotte, I'm not sure if I'd ever get enough.

Eventually, she pulls away and rests her forehead against mine and smiles wide. We both do.

"How about this," I say, "we could take it one day at a time and see where things go. If we get back to New York and we don't want to see each other anymore, then we don't. I know you're a busy woman and your career is important to you, so if you feel like spending time with me is taking away from that, we'll hit pause and wait until things settle down."

"What if I want to make time for you?" she asks.

I smile. "Well, I guess we'll see where it goes, then."

She squeezes my hand again. "I'd like that."

"First thing's first, though. We need to make amends with your family."

She drops her gaze to the floor. "Yeah, I suppose you're right. It's not over yet."

"Let's go."

I lead her out to the dining room where the rest of her family is gathered around the table. The steaming casserole is sitting in the center untouched.

"Finally!" Jim exclaims. "We can eat!" He reaches for the spatula.

"In a minute," I say. "Charlotte has something she needs to say."

He sets the utensil down and looks up at her. "I thought we squared this away earlier?"

"I just wanted to apologize again for lying," Charlotte says. "To everyone."

"Oh, honey." Maria gets up and comes around the table to hug her daughter. "Don't beat yourself up over this. I'm sorry for pressuring you. Your father and I talked and we'll come out to visit you in the spring."

"Yeah, maybe we can have Easter there," Olivia suggests.

"That'd be a little tough with the kids," Arthur mutters.

Olivia gives him a death stare. "We'll figure it out, *sweetie.*"

"Guys, it's okay," Charlotte says. "I just want to be able to share my accomplishments—all of them—with you guys. Right now, that's mostly in my career." She grins. "But I think that might be changing a bit in the near future."

"What do you mean?" Olivia asks.

I look down to hide my grin, but it's too obvious.

"Ah," she says.

"Come sit down and have something to eat." Maria ushers us to the table. "The food's getting cold. We've already said our apologies and we're going to make some changes, but Christmas isn't over yet. There's still time to celebrate!"

Charlotte and I take our seats and start filling our plates. Jim sits back and studies us as he chews on his dinner roll.

"So where do things stand for you two?" he asks.

"You're welcome to stay the rest of the week, Kaden," Maria offers.

"Thanks." I look over at Charlotte and she smiles back at me. "And I'm not really sure where we stand yet."

Charlotte looks up at me. "We'll figure it out one day at a time."

Pick up *A Christmas Spark*, Small Town Christmas, Book 3!
DavidNethBooks.com/AChristmasSpark

BEHIND THE BOOK:
A Christmas Charade

✳ ✳ ✳

I had the idea for A Christmas Charade since I first wrote A Christmas Reunion. I knew it'd make a good sequel to the first book in the Small Town Christmas series, but I was working on other books and I wanted to write the Montana Beach series, so I didn't get to writing it until July 2018…which happened to be one of the hottest months on record.

Merry Christmas in July, right?

There were days that I was writing about bracing against the cold, drinking warm beverages, and experiencing the homey atmosphere of a small town Christmas while I had multiple fans blowing on me, I was guzzling lots of water to stay cool, and wiping the sweat from my forehead. To get in the mood, I'd light a holiday-scented candle to bring the season's greetings to the surface.

Luckily, the heat passed. I took the break in the weather to look at the story critically, which required a rewrite of the ending. Originally, the book ended on December 23rd and Charlotte and Kaden just kind of spontaneously decided to start dating, with no real resistance from her family.

No conflict, no story.

So I made Charlotte's dad the one to call them out. The thread was already present in the story, so reworking the ending came pretty easy. Actually, I like it better the way it turned out. The story ends with Charlotte and Kaden agreeing to test out a real relationship between them, meaning that both Charlotte and her mom caved a little. Compromise equals a happy ending.

This whole series was inspired by the Hallmark Christmas movies. I like the idea of cute little stories that are perfect for the season. With this book in particular, I wanted to depict a crazy-busy woman returning to her roots and stumbling into love. The basic premise has been done before, but I wanted to put my twist on it with familiar connections to the first book in the series.

Another movie that really inspired this book was "Holiday in Handcuffs." The explosive Christmas dinner in the movie was especially inspiring to me for this story. I tried to add in some cooky characters as well, because every family has a cooky character or two!

I hope you enjoyed reading the second book in the Small Town Christmas series. Please consider leaving a review on the retailer you purchased it from, and don't forget about Goodreads!

Please come home for Christmas...

Tanya Bennett is still feeling the effects of her mental breakdown from last year after her parents died. She lost a lot of loved ones in a short period of time, but most notably her son, who she can't see without supervision. With some help from her friends, she's back on the right track with a new job and volunteering with the school play her son's in. But a bad reputation is hard to overcome and whether she can spend Christmas with her son hinges on how well her upcoming court date goes.

If not for Christmas, by New Year's night...

Adam Allen is still trying to figure out how to co-parent with his controlling ex, who is always quick to criticize his parenting. It doesn't help that he's so forgetful and he works a lot, but at least he's try-ing. It's hard for him to find someone who can relate, until he meets Tanya.

Adam feels an instant connection with her, but her episode the year before has ripple effects that could alter both of their relationships with their kids.

DavidNethBooks.com/AChristmasSpark

More by the Author

To find the rest of the author's books visit
DavidNethBooks.com/Books

Subscribe to his newsletter to be the first to know of new
releases and special deals!
DavidNethBooks.com/Newsletter

If you enjoyed the book, please consider leaving a review on
Goodreads or the retailer you bought it from. Reviews help
potential readers determine whether they'll enjoy a book, so
any comments on what you thought of the story would be very
helpful!

About the Author

D. Allen is the author of the sweet small town romance series, Montana Beach and Small Town Christmas.

Also writes fantasy and superhero fiction as David Neth.

www.DavidNethBooks.com
www.facebook.com/DavidNethBooks
www.twitter.com/DavidNethBooks
www.instagram.com/dneth13

www.ingramcontent.com/pod-product-compliance
Lightning Source LLC
Chambersburg PA
CBHW051704180726

48283CB00004B/1207